NEW YORK REVIEW BOOKS
CLASSICS

CRAZY GENIE

INÈS CAGNATI (1937–2007) was born in Monclar, France, in the Aquitaine region of Lot-et-Garonne, and died in Orsay. The child of Italian immigrants, she became a French citizen but never considered herself French. With a bachelor's degree in modern literature and a certificate for secondary-school instruction, she worked as a professor of literature at the Lycée Carnot in Paris. Cagnati was the author of four prize-winning books: *Le Jour de congé* (*Free Day*, 1973; available as an NYRB Classic); *Génie la folle* (1976); *Mosé, ou Le Lézard qui pleurait* (1979); and *Les Pipistrelles* (1989).

LIESL SCHILLINGER is a literary critic, writer, and translator, and teaches journalism and criticism at the Eugene Lang College of Liberal Arts of the New School for Social Research in New York City. Her articles, reviews, and essays have appeared in *The New York Times*, *The Wall Street Journal*, *The New York Review of Books*, *The New Yorker*, *The Atlantic*, *The Washington Post*, and other publications. She has translated works by Alexandre Dumas fils, Nataša Dragnić, Jean Echenoz, and others, and is the author of *Wordbirds: An Irreverent Lexicon for the 21st Century*. In 2017 she was named a Chevalier of the Order of Arts and Letters of France.

CRAZY GENIE

INÈS CAGNATI

Translated from the French by

LIESL SCHILLINGER

NEW YORK REVIEW BOOKS

New York

THIS IS A NEW YORK REVIEW BOOK
PUBLISHED BY THE NEW YORK REVIEW OF BOOKS
207 East 32nd Street, New York, NY 10016
www.nyrb.com

Originally published in French as *Génie la Folle*.

Library of Congress Cataloging-in-Publication Data
Names: Cagnati, Inès, 1937-2007 author | Schillinger, Liesl translator
Title: Crazy Genie / by Inès Cagnati; translated by Liesl Schillinger.
Other titles: Génie la folle. English
Description: New York: New York Review Books, 2026. | Series: New York Review Books classics
Identifiers: LCCN 2025039189 (print) | LCCN 2025039190 (ebook) | ISBN 9798896230205 paperback | ISBN 9798896230212 ebook
Subjects: LCGFT: Fiction | Novels
Classification: LCC PQ2663.A334 G413 2026 (print) | LCC PQ2663.A334 (ebook)
LC record available at https://lccn.loc.gov/2025039189
LC ebook record available at https://lccn.loc.gov/202

ISBN 979-8-89623-020-5
Available as an electronic book; ISBN 979-8-89623-021-2

The authorized representative in the EU for product safety and compliance is eucomply OÜ, Pärnu mnt 139b-14, 11317 Tallinn, Estonia, hello@eucompliancepartner.com, +33 757690241.

Printed in the United States of America on acid-free paper.
10 9 8 7 6 5 4 3 2 1

To Térésina Stédile, my mother

I

THEY CALLED her Crazy Genie.

Sometimes she walked through the village with her hurried step, on her arm the wooden basket that always held the jute bag she used as a hood when it rained. Me, I ran behind her as fast as my little legs would carry me. If she disappeared around a corner or behind a car, or behind a group of the chattering women of the morning who were doing their shopping, or standing in doorways, gathering water from the rainspouts to water their flowers and wash their sidewalks, the fear would come over me that she would use the opportunity to leave me there, all alone, in that street full of unknown houses, of unknown faces. I wouldn't even have known how to find our old house beside the willows on the river. So I ran as fast as I could on my little legs, with a crazy heart, to catch up with her. Sometimes she stopped for a moment. I would slow down to rest a bit, beaming at her as she waited for me. She always started off again before I could catch up with her. Once more I ran, eyes fixed on her back.

When she walked through the village like this, which was rare because usually, to get to the farms, she went around it by taking side roads or by cutting through the fields, the people fell silent and watched her approach, pass by, and move on. They didn't laugh. They didn't greet her with friendly jokes. She walked along, eyes in the distance, me running after her, and they watched her.

If anyone needed to talk to her, they would say: "Crazy Genie."

Never: "Eugénie."

Nor: "Madame."

Always: "Crazy Genie."

2

SHE WENT to the farms to help with the chores. In winter, she cut the hedges or chopped wood, made up bundles of kindling. On Thursdays I went with her. I gathered the small branches, put them in piles. We were alone. At noon she made a little fire.

I remember the winter woods, the fire, the cold, her and me in the cold woods.

In springtime, she spaded the vines, the fields of green peas, beans. I remember the wild tulips, yellow or red, among the vines. I gathered them, made yellow-and-red bouquets of them for her, which wilted at the end of the rows. I also gathered lamb's lettuce and wild leeks and at night we ate them.

She picked peas or beans. She brought back the ones they gave her in her basket. We ate them. Whatever was left over, she canned.

Harvest season arrived. The countryside filled with fragrance. She came home, her hair covered with dust and bits of hay. There was the weeding of the corn, the crops, the green beans, tomatoes, the harvesting of fruit, and we ate fruit, made jam and more preserves. During the grape harvest, she came back smelling sweet and sticky, and they gave her some of the yellow wine that makes your head spin a little.

She would go to make meals for baptisms, communions, weddings. Sometimes she took me with her. I would stay in the damp kitchens to watch her. She would always say to me: “Get out of my hair.”

I would leave for a while. I would wander a little around the unknown house. Then I would come back to her. Once more she would say: “Get out of my hair.”

I would leave. I would sit against a wall or under a hedge, watching for her to walk out the door. I remember the smells, the sun against the walls, her in the dark kitchens, the sunflowers that revolved in the fields.

3

IN SUMMER, she went barefoot. Her heels were covered in thick, insensitive calluses. In winter, she wore black rubber boots. She stuffed them with straw. The straw stuck together under her feet, forming a hard, damp slab that retained the shape of her foot when she changed it at night. The calluses on her heels broke out in blood-streaked cracks.

Every night before going to bed, she bathed her feet in a basin of warm water, removed the dirty debris lodged in the cracks with a matchstick filed to a point, or a sliver of wood. I would sit by the fireplace to watch her and wait. She would say: "Go to bed."

I would go lie down. She would come to bed. Sometimes, she would hold me against her. Other times, she fell asleep at once, far, far away in the depths of her exhaustion.

4

BACK WHEN I was very little, she took me with her every day to the farms where she worked. In the basket, she carried the jute bag, which she put on the ground at the edge of the fields so I could sit on it. She worked. I played a little with the dirt, with the roots of the quack grass, with the field grasses. I watched her. I was afraid she might go away and leave me there, all alone at the edge of that unknown field.

Some days, the mist rose up from the river, drowned the sad willows, buried the world. Morning never broke. She appeared to me like a shadow that got paler and paler as her work drew her farther away from me. When she was just about to vanish into this milky mist, I would run toward her in the field. Sometimes I stopped as soon as I could see her again. I would advance little by little to keep her in sight. Other times, I went all the way up to her, clung to her skirt, wanting her to hold me for a little while. She would say: "Go sit on the sack."

I would return to the edge of the field as slowly as possible to prolong the time that I could still see her. I would sit down on the sack. She was lost in the depths of the mist. I would stay there looking toward her, waiting for the moment when she would reappear. Time stretched. Once more I would believe she had gone off and left me there because she didn't want me.

I would get up with a crazy heart, I would run toward her as fast as my little legs could carry me, I would fall, get back up, run. I would see her at last. I would sit down on the wet ground. I would have liked to go up to her, to tell her how happy I was that she was still there.

At noon, if the farm wasn't too far away, we went there to eat. We sat down to lunch in dark, damp kitchens. The people talked, she kept quiet. Sometimes the women or the children looked at me, asked me things like my name or my age. I didn't answer, I would cling to her, put my face in her skirt. The women would say to me: "Cat got your tongue?"

And among themselves: "She's like her."

Me, I would cling all the harder to her so she would pick me up. She would push me away a little and say: "Keep still."

If the farm was too far away, we ate in the field. She would take off her boots, sit on a corner of the sack, and we would eat bread and cheese, or bread and sausage, or bread and omelet, sometimes bread and dried autumn fruit. We would drink from the bottle, wine and water for her, milk and water for me. When we had finished, she would put the things away in the basket.

Before returning to work, she would stay for a moment there, close to me, her eyes far-off, to rest a bit, or think of her own things. I would have liked to lean against her. She would get up, put her boots back on, and leave, saying: "Sleep for a while."

I would lie down on the sack and try hard to sleep, like she said. But as soon as my eyes were closed, I would imagine that she would use the opportunity to run away, or even that she would simply leave, forgetting me there. I would get back up and once again search for her shadow in the mist.

When night fell, she would straighten up at last, take

stock of the day's work, look far away toward things that weren't there, then come to me. I would stand up. She would shake out the dirt or the crumpled old grasses from the sack, fold it, and put it in the basket. If there was bread left from midday, she would give me some. She would start walking fast, and me, I would run after her so as not to lose her. She would end up being far ahead. My heart would go crazy. She would finally stop, wait for a while. As soon as I came near her, she would start walking again.

There were also times when she would bend down to me, wipe my face, and carry me in her arms. Then I would put my head in the warmth of her neck and I would cry. Sometimes she would say: "Don't cry."

Most often, she said nothing.

5

OFTEN she cried at night, in front of the fire. Her eyes would take on the color of tears. She would say: "And me, I've had nothing."

I would say: "Me, you have me."

But she would keep on crying. Then I would believe that she didn't want me. I wanted to love her every minute of my life so that she would want me, I followed her everywhere. She would say: "Get out of my hair."

But me, I wanted to love her, to always be near her.

Coming home from school, I would run the whole way down the side roads, in the mud, in the claws of the brambles, in the pink clamor of the quince trees. I would bounce in the potholes. Sometimes I found her at home washing or ironing. I would go to her, transported. For a moment she would let me be near her, and then she would say: "Get out of my hair."

Sometimes she wasn't back from the farms yet. I would stand by the side of the path and wait, watching the evening shadows for her arrival. I remember the empty path whose shadows I scrutinized.

Our evening meal was sometimes fritters, made with apples in winter, with acacia flowers in springtime, with pumpkin blossoms in summer. I would sit by the fireplace, I would watch the too-fierce fire, I would eat the burning-hot fritters. My mouth and fingers were greasy and full of sugar. The house was hot and fragrant.

After dinner, in winter, she would knit. Night gripped the old house. I would think: "She is here."

To push back the night.

Every now and then she would tell a story. She always told the same one, the one about the three young girls, Rose, Daisy, and Violet. The flames leapt up. Would the ogre devour gentle Violet? A night would come when the ogre would devour the beautiful young girl. It depended on her. I would watch her face, bent over her knitting. Her monotonous voice ordered the events of this never-ending story. When she stopped speaking, she would put down her knitting. Sometimes she stroked my cheek. Her light eyes, then, would appease the ghosts.

Other nights she was silent. When I was big enough, I said, so she wouldn't be sad anymore: "One day we will go away, far away, to lands where the vines touch the sky, where we will get lost in forests of acacias in pursuit of wild cyclamens."

She never responded. I knew there couldn't be lands where vines grow up to the sky, where you could lose yourself along the banks of streams while hunting wild cyclamens. I just wanted to console her. When you're little, you don't know.

6

I MET PIERRE one night, at the train station. He came up to me and said: "I am Pierre."

And I: "I am Marie."

This was much later, after the unbearable things had happened and before other things that were to come, a night in December before Christmas. The high school was far away, and me, I was going to her, who was at Antoine's house. The train had stopped in the countryside. At the station, in the night, all the buses, all the trains, had left. I stayed in the waiting room that smelled of crushed cigarette butts, of past waiting.

The stationmaster came and said: "You have to leave. The last train is about to come through. After that, I must close the station."

Me, I said: "I don't know where to go. All the buses have left."

He said again: "You have to leave."

The last train came through. When the travelers dispersed, there was Pierre. The stationmaster came up and said to Pierre: "You have to go. I must close the station."

And Pierre said: "I fell asleep on the train. I have to wait for tomorrow's train to go back the other way."

In the end, the stationmaster locked us inside the station. After a long silence, as I looked at the bare linden trees on the small square while Pierre looked at the empty tracks, he came up to me and said: "I am Pierre."

And I: "I am Marie."

7

WHEN I was little, in the springtime, I often went to my grandmother's to sit beneath the big paulownia tree in front of the house. I would lie down and look at the tree's mauve clusters swinging in the sky. It was the hour of the siesta, and grandmother dozed deep in the shadows, in her big armchair between the fireplace and the armoire.

My grandmother did not like me. Nonetheless, I would go to her house on spring days at the hot hour of the siesta to lie beneath the big blooming paulownia tree and look at its soft clusters in the blue of the sky.

Sometimes my grandmother would be under the tree washing big plaid handkerchiefs, slowly, for a long time.

I would leave. Or I would go look at the old fig tree between the barn and the house. I would climb it and stay motionless for a long time, while my grandmother washed the big plaid handkerchiefs under the mauve clusters of the paulownia.

Other times I would go into the house.

My grandfather was eternally leafing through his books on the little table by the window. I would draw near and wait. Then, because my grandfather didn't see me, I would tug his empty sleeve. I would say: "Grandfather."

He would raise his head, look at me, recognize me, say: "Marie. Little one."

With his only hand, he would fumble in the musette bag that he always wore on a bandolier on the side of his missing arm. He would pull out walnuts, hazelnuts, or an apple from it, put them in my hand, the nuts in their shells, and say: "Eat, little one."

He would turn away and again recede into the books about old dead kings, in the countries of yesteryear. I would leave. I would go behind my grandmother's house, by the tall oak where the cousins' swing hung. I would break the walnuts or the hazelnuts on the edge of the well. I would throw the dead shells into the well.

I would stay a moment looking at the valley, the river in its hollow, first between the poplars that stood like sentries over the waters, then between the willows. I looked at the white sand of the foxes' hill. I would try to see the house between the hill and the willows, and, maybe, her. I would hurtle through the meadows toward the house and toward her. If she was there, she would say: "I don't want you going up there."

I would keep following her around, hoping she would look at me. She would always end by saying: "Get out of my hair."

I would retreat for a moment, then come back. I wanted to be near her. She would say again: "Stop always getting in my hair."

8

Sometimes they gave her clothes, too old or too small, or that they didn't want anymore. When they were very worn-out, which was often, she made rags out of them that she would use in winter to kneel on when she fed the geese or the ducks at the farms. She kept the best scraps to patch her dresses or her blouses. She cut outfits for me out of old dresses or skirts, and at night, in front of the fire, she took the lamp and hung it under the chimneypiece so she could see properly, and she sewed nonstop. Lying in bed, I would watch her. I didn't want to fall asleep before she was in bed with me. I was afraid that, suddenly, she would put her work down on the table and go away, forgetting me there, alone in the old house gripped by crazy willows that talk at night. I would try not to move. If I moved, she would say: "Sleep."

Without turning her head.

When the clothes they gave her were my size and in good condition, I wore them as they were. I knew who had worn them. I felt as if I became the other people. Those days, at school, I didn't talk. When I passed by the houses of the village, disguised this way, the women who sat chattering on the green benches between the pots of geraniums or begonias, said without lowering their voices: "Luckily, everyone is generous to them."

They looked happy.

Sometimes, too, back when I was very little, she would make me a doll out of those rags. The head and body were stuffed with scraps of cloth, the arms and legs with bits of wood. The doll didn't have hair or features. I would carry it with me everywhere. Very quickly it would fall to pieces because it truly was old, worn-out cloth. I had to wait a long time before she would make me another.

9

SHE BROUGHT back baskets of fruit from the farms. She put the apples and the grapes in the attic, the apples on a bed of straw or on racks, the grapes on iron wires attached to the beams. The apples perfumed the house for months. Some fruits dried in the sun, on racks set out on the roof, whole plums, peaches, and apricots that had been opened, their pits removed. The bees hummed around the racks in the scent of sugar. The fruit shriveled, turned brown, hardened, and the bees moved off.

With the other fruit she made jam, from plums, pears, melons, quinces, green tomatoes, sometimes grapes. The autumn days were perfumed by the apples, by the scent of caramelized fruit and sugar. When the jam was put into glass jars, I scraped the slightly burnt jam that stuck to the bottom and sides of the cauldron. The next day she would cover the jars with parchment paper that was very white and crisp, tied with yarn. Next, all the jars were put away in the big armoire.

A sweet, heavy smell lingered all autumn in the corners of the house. In winter, when she had been dead for a long time, we ate the jam.

10

IN AUTUMN, we went to the farms to help with the corn-husking. We left the house after supper. We walked in the night-filled paths, she in front with the lantern that gave her an enormous shadow, me behind, stuck to her shadow and running with all my strength for fear of losing her and remaining alone in the night. If I bumped into her, she said without turning around: "Get off my heels."

We finally got to the farm. There were always a lot of people, a lot of joyful sounds, as if for a party. We got set up in the sheds, alongside or on top of the piles of corn, with crates. We husked the corn, threw the naked ears into crates that the men emptied into the loft or into the dryers.

I would sit up close against her. The people talked, laughed, sometimes sang. She, however, worked in silence, and me, I watched her movements while I played with the old corn silks. Sometimes I fell asleep. I would wake up with starts of terror, I would cling to her. The people would laugh. She would say: "Let me work."

When the piles of corn were done, we ate, everyone ate. We ate boiled chestnuts, pumpkin cake, jam. We drank the new red wine. When we left, they sometimes gave her a basket of corn.

Once again, it was the paths, her in front, me behind, running in the mud.

At the house, she took off her rubber boots, pulled the damp straw out of them, threw it in the fire, and left them gaping open so they would dry. I stayed there watching her. She said: "Go lie down."

In her tired voice. She got undressed and lay down, too. She smelled of straw and warm sweat. Sometimes she held me against her for a moment and said: "You are little."

And immediately I wanted to cry.

II

THE STATIONMASTER had left, the big doors were closed, their glass panels protected by iron in round patterns; the lights were out. The streetlamps on the little square remained, their hazy light penetrating the station.

I was sitting on my bag, at the corner of a wall and a slot machine. Pierre was walking in the murky light. Sometimes he stopped, facing the square with the lonely streetlamps under the pollarded linden trees. Occasionally a train cut through the silence, lost itself far away among the poplar woods and the chattering willows of the rivers. For a long while Pierre walked in the cold and abandon of the night.

Then he stopped in front of me and said: "You mustn't sleep. It is too cold."

I got up and walked, too, from door to door, the doors that opened to the platforms, the doors of the baggage check, the doors that looked out on the little square with the streetlamps under the lindens, the door of the newspaper shop. I walked, my legs stiff. I thought: "All the doors are glass-fronted."

And nothing else. It was so cold, and all the trains had already gone by.

In the end, I sat down again on my bag. I looked at the crumpled candy wrappers on the tiles, the crushed cigarette butts, the blackened patches of chewing gum, the dirty traces of the day's steps.

Pierre came again and said: "You have to walk."

He waited. I got up. He said: "We're going to walk and talk until morning so we don't fall asleep. Each of us will talk for half an hour."

He began to speak.

Over there, far away, there were blue islands, islands perfumed with sand, sea, and sun. His voice traversed the deserts of salt water in the sun, the deserts of cold nights; set next to me islands fragrant with frangipani, red birds around red flowers, caves where the sea sweeps in and gets lost. It brought with it warm nights, as soft as silk, where amorous fireflies glide.

He said: "One day, perhaps, I will take you to the gentle islands where I was born."

I made no reply. There had already been, far from gentle islands, she whom they called Crazy Genie, the abbé all alone on his chair, the mason lying in wait on the paths.

Pierre said: "You must believe it. Things come to pass if you believe in them. The fragrant blue islands are there if you believe in them."

At the end of the night, the stationmaster came back, the sweepers. Before heading off, Pierre came up to me again and said: "I will come get you in La Rochelle."

And then: "I am Pierre."

And I: "I am Marie."

I waited until it was time for the bus, with the sweepers, the buckets of water, the mops. Pierre took away with him the gentleness of the red dawns on the hills where the wind sings in the casuarina trees. I thought: "Forever."

It was an early morning, dawn in a train station invaded by sweepers. The stationmaster came and said: "You should go drink a hot coffee, little one."

I said: "Yes."

But I stayed there. I had no money for coffee. In a moment, the stationmaster came back. He gave me some money: "For coffee and croissants."

I sat down in a corner of the café. I drank the very hot café au lait and ate the croissants. And then, I cried. Trains passed from time to time, stopped sometimes, shrieking, soon left again.

In the end, I stopped crying and left. I remember how cold it was. On the bus, I thought of her whom they called Crazy Genie. I wondered if they still called her Crazy Genie, now that Antoine had taken her into his home.

Somewhere there were gardens of wild orange trees around serene white mansions, sea wind in the palms, Pierre, who had left taking the blue-hued perfume of the islands far away with him.

12

IN WINTER it was hog-butchering time. Every farm, according to its size, butchered one or several pigs. She went almost every day to help. We left in the early morning darkness with our rubber boots stuffed with straw, she in front with the lantern that swung in rhythm with her steps. I would try to put my feet where she had put hers, which forced me to make big, awkward steps. Sometimes my too-big boots got stuck in the mud. I would pull my foot out of the boot, the boot out of the mud, put it back on. I would try to catch up with her. She would be far ahead with the lamp, and me, I would wade in the dark.

Sometimes she stopped a bit to wait for me. She would turn toward me, raise the lamp to illuminate me, say: "Hurry up."

And me, I ran as fast as the mud would let me, and I was full of tears. When I had almost caught up with her, she would set off again.

At last we would arrive at the farm where they were killing the pig. She helped first to milk the cows, to make the fire under the big washtub installed in the shed, to bind the pig's feet, to hang it from the hoist with its head pointing down. She would hold the bucket under the head while the butcher bled it, to collect the blood. The pig screamed. If he took a long time to die and screamed a long time, the man would insult him: "The bastard. He doesn't want to die."

And he would dig into the wound with his knife. She would say nothing, hold the bucket. Me, I watched. Sometimes, if she noticed my presence, she would say: "Get out of here."

But me, I wanted to stay near her.

I remember those muddy early mornings, her holding the bucket where the foaming blood flowed, rivulets of bloody mud, the man who insulted the screaming pig that didn't want to die yet.

All day long she worked. She scalded the pig with buckets and buckets of water, she helped scrape the skin to remove the bristles. She chopped up the meat and the bacon for pâté, sausages, boudin, she salted and rolled up the belly, salted the bones of the salt pork that would be left in a tub and used later to make soups with cabbage or beans. She washed the intestines that were to be filled with sausages, *saucisson sec*, and boudins. She labored unceasingly, in silence, and the people, happy, talked and laughed. Me, I always stayed near her, careful not to impede her movements so she wouldn't notice my presence, to help her if I could. Sometimes, nonetheless, she said: "Stop always getting in my hair."

I would move away a little, then I would come back.

When it was the time for the mailman to come, they would tell me to go look for him and invite him to the midday meal. At noon, the mailman came. Everyone ate pork on the spit, or pork with olives, while talking very loudly.

At the end of the afternoon, they asked her to go muck out the stable. I stood near the barn door and watched her throw out through a little window, onto the manure pile, the cow dung, the straw soaked with urine, spreading in their place a litter of clean and golden straw that still smelled a little of the fields of summer. She cut up beets and distributed them to the animals with the dusty hay.

I waited. If she disappeared behind the mangers or into the hayloft, I was afraid she would never come back, because at times like these, once night had come in the old house at the edge of the willows, she would cry, saying: "And me, I've had nothing."

Me, I would go to her. I would put my head on her knees and say: "Me, you have me."

But she would cry without hearing, her eyes taking on the color of tears.

When she had finished spreading the litter, she had to milk the cows again. She stayed a long time under each one of them, milking her, pouring the milk into the cans. I would move with her from beast to beast, without making a sound, for fear that she would say to me: "Go into the house."

Then would come the evening meal with the greasy smell of unfamiliar dishes, the return to our house. Sometimes she brought things back in her basket, a few sausages, some boudins, a cured sausage, a salty bone to make soup with. She hung the charcuterie up on strings hooked to the ceiling, not far from the fireplace, so it would dry and ripen.

The next day we would return to the farm to help make the lard and the cracklings, to salt the bacon, the ham. Or we would go to another farm. Once more, all day long, in the dirty light of a day that never broke, I would wait for the evening, for the time when the two of us would be in the bed, where I wouldn't need to be afraid anymore, where I wouldn't have to wait for the daylight that wouldn't come.

13

IN WINTER, she went to the woods to make bundles of kindling. Sometimes the woods were far away. On Thursdays, she took me with her. We would leave early, in the desert of pale winter daylight that never breaks. Our breath hung around us in white halos.

She cut the big branches, the little branches. Me, I piled them into heaps, the points all on the same side, orderly. The air smelled of sap and sawdust.

She didn't speak. We were alone, everywhere, in the woods. There was silence, cut by blows of the pruning hook that reverberated in the trees, went off into the distance, extinguished themselves in the land beyond, and I wondered if anyone could hear us, could know that any living creature was alive here.

She, she cut the branches, and me, I piled them into even bundles.

At noon, and she judged the hour by the strength of the daylight, she lit a fire. She made our meal. I sat down and I watched her. On the embers she cooked the sausages that the people had given her when they killed the pig, and the grease sputtered and smoked. In the hot ashes she baked the potatoes, or she warmed the beans or the cabbage. Me, I watched her. Sometimes she said: "Don't get in my hair, watching me."

I gathered twigs or pieces of bark for the fire, without going far. I wanted always to be near her and to watch her.

Once again we worked, and once again there were the sharp blows, the cracking of branches, the rustling of leaves and old ferns echoing far off in the silence. The winter birds fluttered around the fire, stealing crumbs. They remained in a circle around the fire like people telling each other things, tranquilly, on an afternoon by the fireside.

When the light faded, we turned back toward the house. The puddles and the mud slapped against our boots.

One time, it was Mardi Gras. On our way home, she made crêpes. I remember the cold, our numb fingers, the burning of the fire, the scent of vanilla, her and me in the deserted woods making bundles of kindling.

14

SHE TOOK me to mass on Sundays. I remember one Sunday above all. While crossing the square where, on one side, the city hall rises with its monument to the dead of all wars, and, across from it, the church, flanked by boutiques under arcades, she was stopped by the doctor. He said to her: "Genie, I helped you when you had the little one."

He waited for her to recall that distant time when he had helped her and say yes. But she said nothing. She stayed standing in front of him in the silence that always enveloped her. On the square, the people she had worked for, who were going to mass or going shopping, or who had come to the village simply to see other people and chat, had stopped to watch us and listen. As she remained silent, the doctor repeated, more loudly, as if to help her understand: "I helped you, Genie, when you had the little one. Now it is I who need you."

He broke off to give her time to get it into her head what was happening to her. He seemed contented and patient. Everyone around was waiting for what would come next, and the square was plunged into a great, unsettling silence. Me, I wanted to grab her by a fold of her dress and drag her away so we could go far from there. As she still made no response, the doctor explained: "You will come live at my house with the little one, Genie."

He reached out his hand toward my head, and I quickly

hid behind her. He remained with his hand in the air.

"You will have a lovely bedroom with a powder room and a bathroom, Genie. You will do the housework, a little cooking, and receive the patients. You will be fed, and beyond that, you will receive a small salary, a real salary, every month, Genie. You can move in as soon as tonight if you would like."

He stopped speaking and waited for her answer. Me, I was still behind her, hiding and holding her dress with both hands, I leaned around and looked at the doctor.

Suddenly, I was reminded of my grandmother's big rooster. He lorded it over all the chickens, and nobody dared stand up to him, not even the dog, who is, nonetheless, a good dog who barks loudly with lots of scary gestures. And then, one day, the big rooster felt like eating the dog's food, which my grandfather puts in an aluminum plate. The dog, she did not like this, you must never mess with her dinner. She growled, reared up at the same time as the rooster, and in one sole bite, cleanly cut off his head. Just like that, the most terrible thing was when my grandmother found the rooster lying beside its head. I stayed hidden in the fig tree, watching her brandish the rooster in one hand, its dead head in the other, and listening to her threaten the entire world. The whole time, the dog slept peacefully. I would really have liked for my grandmother to be in the rooster's place, but I understood very well that this would have been hard because the dog could not have cut her head off cleanly in one bite.

The doctor waited, and around us everyone waited for what she would decide. She, she stayed motionless for a moment, in front of the doctor. Then she turned around and pushed me toward the church without saying anything. Behind us, the doctor again said: "You can come as soon as tonight, Genie. You will have a real salary."

In the crowd, someone said: "Bravo, Genie. You're right."

But not too loudly. It was better not to say things to certain people, like the doctor, the notary who always walked with his newspaper unfolded in front of him and fell one day into a ditch, the secretary at the town hall who handed out leaflets against bottles of eau-de-vie, or the priest and the police.

At the end of mass, people tried to stop her to tell her: "You did the right thing, Crazy Genie."

Or: "It's no life, being a maid."

Or again: "And us, don't we help you every day, Crazy Genie?"

She kept walking and very soon we found ourselves on the path, she in front, me behind, running as fast as my little legs could carry me so as not to lose her among the brambles.

15

THE WHITE hill behind the house was full of foxes. They had dug dens into the sand everywhere, sometimes open to the sky, sometimes sheltered under the roots of bare bushes. I knew them all from running over the hill. There were also wild rabbits, and in hunting season the village hunters went looking for them and tracked them under the brambles. Foxhunting was always allowed, even during breeding season. They hunted the foxes with guns or traps. In winter, when the countryside was all deserted, the hungry foxes went howling around the farms and supplied themselves with poultry, even from the best-protected farmyards. On moonlit nights, you could hear them barking on the hill and the farm dogs lost their minds.

When someone had killed a fox, he tied its paws together, passed a stick between its four round paws and went from farm to farm so people could thank him for this service rendered to all by giving him some money. More often than not, it was the eldest son of the farm who made the rounds, and as he went along, other children joined him, following him respectfully, him with the fox on his shoulder, like an illustrious personage in a procession.

I remember the flaming auburn of the foxes' fur, their opulent tails, their narrow little muzzles. I remember how much I wanted to tame a fox and for him to be my friend.

But you can't tame a fox. You can only kill it. When you're little, you don't understand.

They also killed magpies. They would throw poisoned kernels of corn into the meadows, into the edge of the woods. The famished winter magpies ate them. I would find them, claws toward the sky, stiffened by death, all over the hill. I would gather them and bury them in a hole in the sand while other magpies screamed from tree to tree.

16

A LONG time after the night at the train station, I found Pierre in La Rochelle. I was walking on the road that stretches along the ocean and the chestnut trees were blooming white or red in the sun. Suddenly, in this flowered sunshine, Pierre was there. He said: "Marie."

Softly, me, I said: "Pierre."

In the golden silence of that day, the wind rocked the clusters of the chestnut trees that looked out on the ocean.

Pierre said: "I called for you everywhere. In the airplane I said your name: Marie."

And me, I was Marie.

He said: "I will take you far away to where I was born, in the blue shade of beaches, on gentle islands of frangipani. I will take you to the edge of the deserts and the jackals will come cry at the moon. The nights will be full of the cries of jackals between the sand and the moon."

And the cries of the jackals became tears of the moon.

17

SOMETIMES I remember the young abbé alone on his chair. It had been, until then, a beautiful month of May. For the procession in honor of the Virgin, the whole village on the hill was a bouquet of joyful celebration. In the avenue that encircled it, they had put up shrines of flowers, of perfumes, of holy images. The chestnut trees swung their soft clusters above the shrines.

Afterward, when everything was over, the shrines withered, the images gone, the village calmed, the policemen silent, I went wandering along the hedges of flowering honeysuckle, or I lost myself in the wild grasses of the ditches. I lay down. The grasses covered me, I rocked myself in clouds.

Often I remember that month of May. I was twelve years old. The village, flowery with shrines, was as bright as a happy voice. The procession twined, harmonious, from village to village, stretching out on roads bordered with wild fennel. It seemed to come from another world with its miraculous Virgin.

Lucette, the daughter of a policeman, and I, we had to decorate the altars of the church. I loved the church, the incense, the sunlight through the stained-glass windows that cast blurry, colored clusters onto the paving stones. I amused myself by putting my face into the patches, red, green, yellow, blue, one after the other, and my face was in succession red, green, yellow, blue. We were in the choir loft, Lucette and I, our arms filled with flowers, playing at putting our faces in the rays of color while we closed our eyes. We laughed. We were happy. We laughed.

When we opened our eyes, the unknown abbé was there.

I was afraid. I should have fled far away from there, thrown away those armloads of useless flowers. I remember how afraid I was and truly I should have fled.

The abbé smiled. He crouched before us, patted our thighs to calm our emotion.

Suddenly, I was happy. He was nice, looked at me, smiled at me, spoke to me gently.

While leaving the church with Lucette, in that bright world, I was still happy. Yes. I remember what a joyful festival it had been until then.

18

PIERRE spoke of Hyères, of airplanes. He talked about the camp on the sea road, the velvety perfume of the mimosas along the avenues bordered with palm trees. He talked about the orange trees in the paths, the green waters and the blue waters of the sea. He said: "Marie. My sweet. My lonely one. My flower."

When he left, he said, on the platform: "Don't feel bad, Thumbelina, I'll be back."

He wrote: "On the plane I say your name: Marie."

And me, I was Marie.

19

THERE was a midnight mass in honor of the statue of the Virgin that people were carrying from village to village.

She had sewn a dress for herself and one for me of the same flowered cloth, decorated with red ribbons. We were in the church that night, in our flowered dresses, me all close to her and happy to look like her. The singing formed a harmonious cathedral around the Virgin who held out her open hands.

That's when the police came looking for us in the church and everything changed forever.

They led us out of the song-filled church, in our new flowered dresses. At the police station, a lot of other policemen were waiting for us, some priests and the young abbé of the afternoon.

Lucette's father wanted me to tell what had happened in the church, in the afternoon. I told. Everybody listened. A policeman wrote. When I had finished, Lucette's father told me to start over, to remember all the details, to remember well. I remembered and I spoke of the armfuls of flowers to decorate the altars, our faces in the colored clusters of sunshine, the young abbé who crouched before us, who patted our thighs to calm our anxiety, all the joy where I was.

When I had finished, I had to start all over again. I told again of the smile, the gentle voice, the hand that calmed.

They questioned again. What had the young abbé done to us, precisely, with his hand. The police, the priests, interrogated nonstop, all night and all the next morning. Me, I said: "No. He didn't do anything."

I said again: "No. He didn't do anything. He spoke in his smiling voice, he patted our thighs, and me, I was so happy."

The abbé kept quiet, all in black on his chair.

She, she had fallen asleep on the bench in her dress that had gone all wilted.

I remember the abbé all alone on his chair, her asleep on the bench in her new dress that was all wilted, her hands hanging limply.

20

ON THE way to the high school, I always passed the same sweeper who swept the sidewalks with his besom broom. He would stop when I passed and say: "Good morning, little bouquet of springtime."

Often I think of that man.

Pierre was supposed to come. It was the time of winter dawns, when the light air, of the pale purplish shade of blue of certain lilacs, softly enveloped things.

Pierre came. I fell asleep bathed in warm night in a red explosion of bitter pomegranate.

Pierre left. I accompanied him to the station. On the platform, beside the Hyères train, he said: "You must go, Thumbelina."

I still stayed. He said: "My Thumbelina. My sweet. Don't cry. I'll be back. I will take you far away, to the blue sand of blue islands, to the song of the casuarina trees."

He said: "We will walk in the paths of wild orange trees. We will sleep in the garden of grapefruits in the shade of bitter perfumes."

I left Pierre. I went out into the sickly light of streetlamps, the cigarette butts, the dirty trampled papers. I sat down on the steps in the courtyard of the station. It was cold everywhere. Far away in the train Pierre said: "My sweet. My lonely one. Don't cry. I'll be back."

21

AFTER the night of the policemen, there were the journalists. They interrogated and interrogated. What had the young abbé done to us. Me, I said: "No. No."

But they interrogated. What was it that the young abbé had done to us, then.

I spoke again: the church, the armfuls of flowers, our happy faces in the colored clusters of sunshine, and then the young abbé suddenly in front of us, the fear, the abbé who spoke in his smiling voice, crouched before us, patted our thighs to calm our anxiety. And I told them of all the joy where I was, somebody had seen me, smiled at me, spoken to me gently in a smiling voice. I remember how much I wanted to say all that, that joy of coming out of the church in bloom.

And the police, the journalists, interrogated again. The young abbé had done something to us because Lucette had said so. I said: "No. No."

And I told just everything, the church, the flowers, the clusters, the gentle voice, all the joy. And I said: "No. No. He didn't do anything."

She slept on the bench in her new dress that had become all rumpled. I remember her hands.

In the newspapers there were photos. Her in her rumpled, flowery dress, asleep on her bench. There was also, in the papers, me, sitting on my chair in my flowery dress that was rumpled like hers, surrounded by policemen and priests. And also there was the photo of the young abbé all in black on his chair.

When at last I left the police station, the young abbé stood up and said: "You're a good little girl, Marie."

And he rested his hand on my head, and me, I looked at him.

In the papers there was a photo of the young abbé leaning toward me, his hand on my head and me, I was lifting my face to him. Beneath the photo they didn't put the abbé's words: "You're a good little girl, Marie."

They put: "And Marie declared how much she enjoyed the experience."

They wrote lots of things in the newspapers. She, who had no husband, yet was the daughter of a respected family, and nobody had ever known who my father was. I, who was left home alone when she hired herself out to people who mostly didn't pay her and she didn't ask to be paid, I, who was left to my own devices in an ancient shack at the foot of a wild hill inhabited by foxes. She, whom people called Crazy Genie, who didn't talk, didn't answer when she was questioned. I, who declared how happy I was with this experience. They wrote a lot of things like that in the papers, and there were these photos:

Her, eyes closed, asleep on the bench in her flowered dress that was all rumpled.

Me, sitting on my chair, my little legs dangling, in my dress that was flowery like hers and also all rumpled, surrounded by priests and policemen.

The young abbé all alone in his black cassock.

The young abbé leaning toward me, his hand on my head,

and me, my face lifted to him when he said: "You're a good little girl, Marie."

And the newspapers said, beneath the photo: "And Marie declared how much she enjoyed the experience."

After that, there was also my grandmother, who came out under the paulownia with the soft mauve clusters in the sky and who said: "You are worse than her."

I never went under the paulownia again.

And there was, the year after that night of policemen and journalists, the mason who haunted the paths.

22

OFTEN, I got to school too early. I waited in front of the courtyard gate for the time when one of the teachers would open the gates. It was so cold.

I would come from the back of the narrow paths between the hedges with dirty boots, my beret, and numb fingers. She would already be at work, far away, by the farms.

At school there were the girls from the town and the girls from the country. The town girls arrived just as the bell rang for start of school. They were in nice clean city shoes, in neat smocks, and their cheeks were rosy with the warmth they had barely left. Sometimes they were finishing eating a piece of buttered toast, in line in front of the classroom door. Among them was Lucette, the policeman's daughter who had lied about the abbé all alone on his chair and who hadn't spoken to me any more since then. The ones from the country lived on the edge of the roads that twined along the border of the properties from farm to farm. They arrived, the big ones in front, the little ones behind. The ones who lived farthest away picked up the others and the groups got bigger and bigger all the way to school. Along the way, they played, told each other secrets, planned outings. They arrived, cheeks red with excitement, their shoes still fairly clean. Sometimes, they had picked lilacs or mock-orange blossoms or other flowers from the gardens at the side of the road to give to the teacher. At hog-butchering time, they brought sausages or roast pork to the teacher; in fruit time, some strawberries, cherries, or peaches; in early autumn, new wine or some of the grapes that are preserved in winter; at Christmas, a fowl. One day, a girl had brought a pullet and it had run away. She had run after the pullet with some of the others to catch it. They arrived, dirty and triumphant, late in the morning, with the plucked fowl. They laughed. The teacher said nothing and gave us a lesson on birds' feathers, their coverts, flight feathers, down, and all that.

Me, I came from the back of the narrow paths between the hedges, with, in winter, dirty boots and numb fingers. In class I couldn't make my stiff fingers write anymore.

The teacher made me rewrite my homework in the notebook, but I was too cold. She showed the others my dirty notebook, to me, she showed a clean notebook. Nobody said anything.

23

WHEN PIERRE came, he brought big bouquets of marigolds. Orange marigolds, yellow marigolds. I put them in the carafe. Their fleshy perfume haunted the air. Long after his departure they lingered, like Pierre's sun, like Pierre's scent, in the house.

At night, he said: "I will take you to the islands where I was born. The paths of wild orange trees lead to the edge of grottoes populated by birds. I will take you to the gentle islands where the birds fly red in the blue skies."

And I was a red bird in a blue sky, a bird nesting in the depths of the caves.

24

BROAD stands of Chasselas grapevines bloomed behind my grandmother's house. In springtime, the scent of their flowering clusters came to meet me along the empty paths from school, between the pale willows of the river, in the grasses of the meadows. In autumn, I went to watch the flight of the bees, motionless, buzzing amid the golden rows and the blue shadows. I ate the grapes that were browned by the sun.

When I got home, if she was there, she said: "I don't want you going up there."

And then I would go back there, on other days, at the hour when my grandmother dozed in the vast wicker armchair between the fireplace and the armoire. I would watch the velvety bees again, I would eat the grapes gilded with sugared sun. She would say again: "I don't want you going up there."

I remember most of all the fragrance of the vines between the pale willows of the river, the golden and blue vines, stretching through the autumn days, haloed by the buzzing of bees flying in place.

25

SHE DIDN'T want me to play like other children when we were on the farms. I didn't understand these things, back when I was very little, or why she would say: "We are not here to play."

I wanted to jump rope. In the schoolyard, under the lindens and the chestnut trees, on the sidewalks in the village, on the farm paths, everywhere, children jumped, on two feet, or hopped, on one, with their jump ropes. Sometimes I stayed and watched. I didn't have a jump rope.

Then, there was that long-ago day when I did have a jump rope. It was a day of sugared almonds for baptisms or weddings, flowery with music or white communion flowers.

She was working in a damp kitchen. I stayed near her by the stove. I followed her if she went out, running on my little legs so as not to lose her. I clung to her skirt. She said: "Leave me alone."

Or: "Go outside."

Then I went out and sat on the ground facing the door so I could still see her, monitor her steps. I remember all the emptiness of the farmyards.

One day, when I was sitting like that, absorbed in watching for her and playing with the dirt a bit, someone came and handed me a jump rope.

It was a very beautiful jump rope with colored wooden

handles. I jumped rope in the farmyard, jumped, jumped again. The jump rope danced in circles like wings, the water of the stream jumped, the sun jumped.

She came, took the jump rope, went back into the house, saying in her weary voice: "We're not here to have fun."

I stayed there, sitting facing the door, and resumed my watch. She came back to bring me creamed cabbage, still warm. I remember that day.

26

PIERRE said: "Over there, you swim at night in water as soft and warm as silk. The fireflies of the water spangle the waves, dance the dance of stars of the water.

"I will take you there, to where I was born, among paths of wild orange trees, where the giant sage plants scream red, and you walk, plunge into them, and lose yourself.

"I will lead you to the edges of the towns. Almost as soon as the rice harvest is over, the sad waters of the swamps cover themselves in water hyacinths. You walk on the narrow banks in a forest of giant clusters of pinkish mauve, the color of certain lilacs."

Pierre talked. His eyes became velvety beaches where star-filled water danced. In the deserted station, his eyes velveted over with the sun of the beaches. I was, at night, on the edge of the beaches, a red bird amid the music of the wind in the casuarinas.

27

AFTER the midday meal, out at the farms, there was a rest period, generally an hour, sometimes more, sometimes less, depending on the season or the farm. During this time of rest, in summer the people vanished into the bedrooms, the dogs into the straw of the barns or out by the streams. In winter the women stayed by the fire doing nothing or knitting, the men and the dogs went into the barns to do I don't know what.

She, she sometimes would sit in the shed by the barn, a little stooped with fatigue, her hands hanging limply in the hollow of her dress. But mostly, they asked her to do things. They would say to her then: "Crazy Genie, since you've got nothing to do . . ."

Or else: "Crazy Genie, while you're resting a bit . . ."

Or again: "Crazy Genie, it would be a bit of a break for you to . . ."

She made no response and prepared to do what they commanded, while each of them went off to lie down or sit. The chores of the siesta were quite varied.

She went into the fields to gather big armloads of beet leaves, or baskets of pears, or apples to give to the pigs who were always ravenous. In summer, she shelled white beans, topped and tailed green beans. In winter, she sorted the lentils, the kidney beans, or the dried peas and took out the ones that had been attacked by weevils. Me, I helped her in silence so she wouldn't say to me: "Get out of my hair."

She cleaned the hen coops or the rabbit cages, burned straw there to exterminate vermin. If a cow was giving birth, she would install herself in the barn on the three-footed stool to monitor the progress of events while the others slept. I would stay near her watching the cow who lowed with pain and watched us with pleading eyes. Sometimes, the little calf was born while we were there. If he was small, this was quickly done. The tips of his heels came first. You had to grab them, pull a little, disengage the head, and after that he came out on his own. Then we would put him on fresh straw near his mother so she could lick him, and we would wait for her to expel the placenta. When the farmer got up, she would say: "It's a male calf."

Or: "It's a female calf."

And she would go off to the fields, and me, I was always very relieved to leave those houses.

If the calf was big, you had to wake the farmer. You attached ropes to the calf's front hooves and pulled until the thorax emerged. If it didn't, the calf would suffocate. Everyone would shout, and me, I would be very scared because the little calf would stick out a long purple tongue. Once the calf was born, the farmer would say: "That's artificial insemination for you. It makes the calves too big."

If we couldn't pull the calf out of his mother's belly really fast, it would die of suffocation. They would bury him. People would be in a bad mood because that was a big loss.

On other farms they made her lead cows in heat to the bull. They would say to her: "That will be a nice outing for you."

There were few bulls and it was always the same place we

went, her in front pulling the cow by the halter, me behind, pushing her with a stick, because cows in heat are always very nervous. We tied the cow to a tree, the man let go the bull, who leapt onto the cow. I was very afraid, always. The farmer said things while he watched her, she, she didn't say anything and as soon as the bull had finished jumping on the cow and began to eat grass, we left again, her in front, me behind.

If the cat or the dog had babies, they would say to her: "Crazy Genie, while you're resting, go kill the kittens."

Or the puppies. She would put kittens or puppies in a sack with rocks and go throw the whole thing into the river. I would follow her, at a distance, because every now and then she would turn around and say: "Go away."

On some farms they buried kittens and puppies alive in the manure piles. I remember the bitches looking for their little ones and crying. They ran everywhere, called, searched, nose forward, for hours. In the end, they crouched in a corner of the house and cried. The people made them omelets with parsley, to stop the milk, and the dogs cried.

If there was an epidemic of myxomatosis, they said to her: "Since you have nothing to do, Crazy Genie, you could kill the sick rabbits."

The sick rabbits were covered with big red sores on their heads, eyes, mouths, ears, noses. They kept their swollen, purulent eyelids shut. They drooled. Above all, they had a way of gently, endlessly moaning, in the little voice of the sick rabbit. People kept the sick mothers until they died, because if they got better, their little ones would be immunized. If they were good to eat, infected young rabbits were killed, you threw away the head and ate the body. You only killed and threw away the very sick rabbits who could no longer eat because they had so many red sores on their mouths. That's the work they had her do. With the flat of her hand, she gave the dying rabbit a great clout to the back of the head. The rabbit, already full of pain and sorrow, emitted a little cry and died.

I said: "Don't do that."

She said: "Shut up."

Or: "Don't watch these things."

When they woke up, the people stretched with contentment and said: "A little nap does you good. Isn't that right, Crazy Genie."

She didn't respond and went off to the fields.

28

SOMETIMES in the evening, she would stay in front of the fire, motionless, her hands hanging limply. I would look at her hands. She would say: "And me, I've had nothing."

I would say: "Me, you have me."

She would cry. She would stretch her old hands toward the fire.

And then, one night, well before Antoine came looking for her to take her to his house, someone knocked on the door. She opened it. It was Louis, the mayor, who came. He said: "I've come looking for you, Crazy Genie. They've taken my wife to the hospital. You've got to take care of the children and the animals."

She said nothing. Then he spoke again: "It's for three months. I'll give you anything you want."

They fell silent, he to let her think it over.

Outdoors it was raining hard. At last she said: "It will be a female calf."

He thought for quite a while. I thought he would refuse because he was known for his stinginess. But he decided: "You shall have the calf. But you must come at once."

They went off in the rain, her head protected by the jute sack used as a hood.

I sat down on the chair beside the door and started waiting. I listened to the sounds of the rain and of the night. I searched my mind for a name for the calf the mayor was going to give her. I thought of Rose, because the daughter of the road repairman you see sitting on all the embankments is named Rose, how pretty she is, and as sweet as a flower, and a person's first name matters to everybody. Outside it was still raining.

Late at night came the wet sound of her steps in the mud. I opened the door very fast. I would have liked to leap into her arms because I was so happy, so happy, that she had finally come back.

She said: "Go to bed at once."

She came back without the calf. I thought that she or the mayor had changed their mind. She went to bed right away, and almost immediately was asleep. She smelled of wood smoke. Just before completely falling to sleep she said: "We'll have to make a place for her in the shed."

Then I was happy again, and again thought about the name I would give her, and that I would go look at the names of the saints on the calendar at my grandfather's house.

I went to consult my grandfather's calendar the next evening, on the way back from school. It was still raining. When she saw me, the grandmother said: "You're just like her. You think of nothing but fooling around."

I stayed anyway, because of the calf we were going to get—she definitely had to have a name—and because I was little. I went to the table where my grandfather was reading the history of crazy old kings in his big books and I said: "I would like to see the calendar."

He took some nuts from his musette bag and said: "Eat, little one."

And after a moment: "I don't think she fooled around. She was a good little girl. But there was a misfortune."

I began looking at every name on the calendar and saw that many of them meant nothing, or if they meant something, it didn't suit the calf we were going to get. In the end, I made up my mind. I gave the calendar back to the grandfather and told him, to thank him: "We're going to get a calf. Her name will be Rose."

He looked at me and said: "That's a great thing, little one. An animal in the house, that's a great thing."

And he resumed reading his big, leather-covered books. When I was near the door, he spoke again: "I'll give you a dog, little one."

I walked slowly toward the house in rain that landed like music on my beret. I thought about the dog and the name I would give it, and of the calf who would be called Rose. I thought: "All three of us will wait for her to come back."

The mud on the path slapped loudly against my boots. Then I had another idea. In the spring I would also get a little duck. He would be called Benoît. And I ran very fast to the house wishing for spring to be here. She hadn't come home yet. I began to wait for her, so I could tell her all the things I was thinking about.

29

On thursdays, if she wasn't home and if she didn't take me with her, I sometimes went to my grandmother's house. Often uncles, aunts, or cousins were there. I would go inside. The faces would turn toward me, fall silent, turn back toward my grandmother, who would say: "She's come to spy on us."

I would wait on the doorstep. The smell of fresh coffee and waxed furniture stupefied me.

The cousins, the uncles, and the aunts didn't talk to me, and they didn't talk to her, either. Nobody knew who my father was, and with me, misfortune had entered the finest family in the region.

My grandfather would finally raise his eyes, the color of the happy summer sky, from his books full of stories of old kings who'd gone mad, and say: "Come, little one."

I would go to him amid the silence of the others. He would burrow with his only hand in the musette bag that hung from the side of his missing arm. He would pull out walnuts, hazelnuts, or an apple, give them to me, saying: "Eat, little one."

Then he would return to his kings who'd been dead forever, or to the story of Dante's journeys in hell, of men who had turned into trees or snakes. I would wait next to him for a while. He would read. I would leave, while my grandmother and her visitors kept mum. As soon as the door closed, the voices rose, the little spoons clinked against the porcelain.

I would go behind the house, near the well. I would eat the apple, the hazelnuts, or the walnuts, which I broke with a stone on the edge of the well. I would throw the apple core or the shells into the well.

Sometimes the grandmother came over by the well to see what I was up to. I would walk slowly until the hedges of the paths hid me. She would wait until I had disappeared before returning to her big house.

I would go up the hill of foxes' sand and wait.

30

PIERRE wrote: "We will go to Oberammergau when the lindens are in flower again."

Pierre came.

At Oberammergau the fragrance of the blooming lindens roved outside the town along the roadways, lost itself far off between the mountains. At night, crazed dogs barked at the sky, men quested in the unbearable scent of the flowering lindens.

Pierre left. At the train station he said: "Marie. My Thumbelina. Don't cry. I'll be back."

He wrote: "I will always go to you, just as the ocean at the end of the world goes to the land."

I remember the cold, on the steps, in front of the train station.

31

THE FIRST night, the mason was on the path, sitting under the big cedar by the bend. He was whistling. He didn't say anything, kept whistling as he watched me pass. I walked on, and when I was far enough away, I ran to the house. She wasn't there. I waited a long time at the edge of the path.

From that day on, he came back on other evenings. He was always sitting calmly under the cedar, watching me pass, while whistling the same tune. I would walk on. Sometimes, at the end of the path, I turned around. He would be whistling, turned toward me. In the end, I stopped being afraid.

Then, one day, when I arrived at the bend where he was whistling, sitting under the cedar, he looked at me as usual, but stopped his whistling. I reached him and he said: "Hello, cutie."

And then he resumed whistling. Then I was afraid again, and when I was far away among the pink-flowered quince hedges, I ran and ran toward the house and toward her, who was not yet back from the mayor's farm.

To wait for her that night, I didn't go onto the path. I climbed up the hill. I stationed myself behind clumps of bushes, where I could monitor the path. I played with the foxes' crumbled sand by the edge of the dens.

32

PIERRE wrote: "You are my sunlit country. I love you for opening the seasons and the roads to me."

Pierre came. The fleshy scent of marigolds filled the air. He laughed. He said: "We must laugh because you are Marie and because I am Pierre."

He said: "We will go look at the sea."

At Ostend, the sea was gray, the sky was gray, the dunes were deserted. We walked with gray dunes ahead of us, gray dunes behind us. We stopped in a hollow of the sand, sheltered from the wind. He said: "My wife. My earth. I will lead you to the shores of seas where the green water is as soft as silk."

Pierre left again. On the platform at the station alongside the Hyères train, he pulled me to him. I became his life in tears.

"Thumbelina. My flower. My sweet. Don't cry. I'll come back."

I waited, sitting on the steps in front of the station until the train left. The train left. Hopes scattered. I waited.

33

SHE GOT up very early to go work at the mayor's house. She started the fire, made the coffee, warmed milk. She cut up little pieces of bread and put them in our two bowls. She poured milk and coffee in hers, sat in front of the fire and ate, her eyes fixed on her bowl. Next, she put the bowl in the sink, went to look for straw, and stuffed her boots with it before putting them on. I watched all her movements from bed. Before leaving, she said: "Sleep a little longer."

I stayed a little longer in the chilled bed then got up in the sad morning. I repeated her movements to make breakfast, fan the fire, do the dishes. I swept the room and threw the sweepings outside if the weather was dry, into the fire if it was raining. Then I waited, sitting by the fire, until it was time to leave for school.

I left for school. The paths between the bare hedges were full of muddy water where I got stuck. I had to pull my feet out of the mud, one after the other, with each step. Sometimes the boots, which she bought too big so they would last longer, stayed stuck in the mud. I would put my foot in the water, pull out the boot, pull out the foot, put my wet foot into the boot. I would move forward. Again I would get stuck, I would pull out the boot, the foot, the other boot, the other foot.

When at last I reached the road, my face, my hands, and

my feet were covered with mud and tears. I would wash my hands and face in the water of the ditches. My feet swam in the sticky water of the boots. I would wash them at night, when I got home.

At night, I lit the fire, warmed myself. I waited for her to come back while listening to the noises the river willows made in the night. Sometimes I opened the door to watch the shadows she would emerge from. If it was raining, I would entertain myself by making my hands into a shell under the gutters to gather water and I would smell its scent of dead leaves and decomposing moss. She didn't come. I went back in. I sat again by the fire and I waited.

Finally, late in the night, I heard the wet sound of her steps. I ran to the door, I opened it for her, filled with joy.

On the embers she heated up the dinner she had brought back for me from the mayor's house. I ate. She said: "Don't eat too fast."

Her damp clothes steamed. She brought back with her the sour smell of the ducks and geese she had force-fed before coming back.

I went to bed. She cleaned her feet, prepared her boots, went to bed. Very quickly, she fell asleep. I thought for a moment of the night when she would bring back Rose, the calf; of the duck, Benoît, that I would have in the spring. I searched for a name for the puppy that my grandfather had promised me. I said to myself: "It will be Ash."

Because an ash tree is full of movement.

34

It sometimes happened that, for a long time, I wouldn't see my grandfather on the paths anymore. I would know then that he had gone off on one of his faraway visits. The day of his departure, he would suddenly lift his eyes from his old books covered in worn leather that told the story of old kings of yesteryear, dead forever, or gone mad, or marooned in the depths of distant years. He would say: "I'm off to see the pope."

Or: "I'm going to Mycenae to see Agamemnon."

Or: "I'm going to Istanbul to see Hagia Sophia."

Or other things like that. And off he would go with, on the side of his missing arm, his musette bag a little heavier than usual, his stick in his hand. He would pause a moment in front of the big house that dominated the valley, under the paulownia or near the cypresses, whose planks he wanted to be buried in, he said. He would look off into the distance. Then he would set out.

Me, I pictured him covering long routes by foot that led to Istanbul, to Epidaurus, to Ithaca. I thought he would meet unknown children, that he would say to them: "It's you, little one."

As he did to me, and that he would give them walnuts, hazelnuts, or an apple. And the children, motionless and stupefied, would watch him head off down other bramble-lined paths.

35

WHEN THE wind blew hard through the branches of the chestnut trees, a rain of petals misted the air. The red chestnuts rocked the white chestnuts in their branches.

In springtime, when I was little, I would lie down beneath the grandmother's big paulownia to look at the mauve clusters swinging gently in the sky. I remember. I dreamed of a man who would take me into his branches, like a tree.

Pierre came. He said: "Marie. My flower. I will take you far away, to the gentle islands of frangipani. The poincianas bloom red and their petals rain blood drops in the wind. I will lead you to the garden of grapefruits and we will sleep far away, deep in islands rocked by oceans."

36

WHEN SHE went to go work at the mayor's, she left very early in the morning, telling me: "Sleep a little longer."

And me, I couldn't sleep. I got up, I repeated her movements, eating the bread in the café au lait, my eyes resting on my bowl, sweeping the room and throwing the trash in the fire or outside in the dirty early morning, doing the dishes or taking water from the cistern. I waited until it was time to go to school, sitting on the stone of the hearth, my back to the fire.

On Thursdays, I went to work on the farms as well. She would say, as she left: "The branches need gathering at Bordeneuve."

And all day long I would make up bundles in the vineyard while the farmer, a bit farther away, pruned the base of the vines with his shears, so the wild tulips could push through their pointy buds. At night, before going home, I gathered leeks or wild lamb's lettuce.

Or else she would say: "They're killing the fattened geese at Moulin du Pech."

And I would pluck the geese, taking care not to tear their skin, swollen with yellow fat. I separated the hard feathers that were to be thrown away from the downy ones that would be kept for eiderdowns and pillows. The women talked.

Or again she would say: "They're killing the pig at Fournier."

I would wash out the intestines for the sausages, the saucisson sec, the boudins, I cut up the pieces of meat, I watched the fire that heated the water of a big cauldron, in a shed. The people talked and laughed. At noon, we ate pork on the spit. The mailman was invited. The people talked and laughed in the house that was damp and full of greasy odors. At night, I went home with, sometimes, things they'd given me—sausages or boudins—or promised, wood, oats.

At home, I would light the fire. I would wait for her to come back, sitting by the door, or standing outside. I awaited her step amid the noises of the night, the willows of the river, the cries from the foxes' hill.

She came home very late, always, carrying with her the sour smell of the fatty, force-fed geese. She warmed the meal that she brought back for me. I ate. She said: "Don't eat too fast."

We went to bed and she fell asleep at once.

Sometimes on Thursdays there was no work for me on the farms. I awaited her return from the moment she'd left the house. To make the time of her absence pass, I washed the kitchen with big buckets of water until the old tiles were clean and gleaming. I set up a corner in the shed for Rose, the calf; for the duck, Benoît; and for Ash, the dog. I stopped up cracks with sacks, I moved the woodpile, I leveled the floor, I cleaned the crates. I went up on the hill of foxes' sand to gather heather, ferns, leaves from the bushes, to make bedding. I wanted Rose, Benoît, and Ash to be happy with us. I also walked along the paths and the banks, beside the streams, seeking patches of tender grass where I could lead the calf to graze. I looked for the spots where the streams would be deep enough to retain water in summer. Benoît would swim there, Rose would drink there, Ash and I, we would watch them, happy.

I went back toward the house, making the journey last as long as possible. From afar, on the hill where I wandered, I looked at the roof of the house, dirty with old moss, the decrepit facade, the chimney without smoke. I always hoped that on that day, the mayor wouldn't have needed her, that when I opened the door I would find her lighting the fire, and me, I would go to her and tell her at last how happy I was that she was there. How happy I was.

I went down the hill of white sand at a run. She was never home.

Sometimes, I couldn't stand anymore to be waiting for such a long time with only the rustling of the river willows. Then I would go toward the mayor's farm, avoiding the paths so nobody would see me. I skirted the wheat fields, crossed the plowed land that was still dotted with old cornstalks from the last autumn. I arrived at the farm.

I climbed the boundary wall, I sat astride it and surveyed the doors of all the buildings, of the barn, the pigsty, the chicken coops, the sheds, the house. She would always end up coming out. I knew she didn't want me to be there, but I didn't hide. If she saw me, she stopped and said: "Go back home."

Then she resumed her work.

I would stay a while longer on the wall and then leave. I would stop in the ditches to wade in the water and wash my boots. While passing by the farms, I looked at the barnyards to see where I could get the little duck Benoît most easily. It was cold. I went home at nightfall. I lit the fire and I waited.

One night, while waiting for her, I sat astride the chair, back to the fire, head leaning on the seat back. I wanted to look like the people in the village.

At the end of summer afternoons, the men of the village

bring chairs out to the threshold of their doorsteps, sit astride them, talk with their neighbors. Sometimes they call out to people who are passing, who stop and also sit for a moment on the doorsteps. The women, on the green benches that lean against the facades, tell each other stories in low voices. The cats and dogs are on or under the benches. The geraniums bloom red at the edge of the windows and at the bottom of the walls. Everyone seems happy to be there, calmly settled on the benches or straddling the chairs, chattering or talking about nothing.

So I had sat that way to look like all those people in the village. I started listening to the sounds of the falling night. And then I fell asleep.

When I woke up, with a jolt and a crazy heart, the fire was dead, the kitchen was full of night, she hadn't come back yet. I was very afraid. Maybe she had come back and, seeing me peacefully asleep on my chair, she had set off again far away, abandoning me forever in the house lost at the back of the land, under the willows.

I went out into the night, I ran with all my strength down the path. I ran and ran, very far, toward her. In the end, there was a shadow. It was her. I stopped and I cried. She said nothing.

At the house, she relit the fire, warmed my supper, emptied her boots of their straw, cleaned the cracks in her heels with a matchstick. In the bed, I was cold and still afraid, and yet, she was there. Before falling asleep, she said: "The calf's horns are growing."

Then, again, I started to cry and cry. She said nothing and then she fell asleep, far, far away.

37

AFTER the night when he'd said to me "Good evening, cutie," the mason had stopped being there, sitting under the cedar by the bend, endlessly whistling. When I came home from school, when I saw that he wasn't there, I stopped a moment to take a good look all around. I sat down, calmly breathing in the cool wind that rustled in the needles of the cedar. I had time. She was still working at the mayor's house and wouldn't be home before the middle of the night.

Afterward I walked home, drinking in the perfume of the wild fennel in the ditch.

Other nights, I sat again under the cedar to listen to the wind, and again I walked calmly in the paths, without hurrying, amid the fragrance of the fennel. Sometimes I even stopped at the edge of the wheat fields to gather a bouquet of little wild gladioli. I went back to the house, I put them in the jug, on the table. Then I waited at the edge of the path for her to come back until late in the night. The crazy willows of the river shook.

On the last of these nights, I took a detour to go look at the mock-orange bushes in the prettiest garden in the village. I stopped in front of the green bars of the gate, and I looked at them from afar. Then, it was such a mild evening, and I was so happy, I came closer, right up to the gate. When you're little, you don't know certain things. To avoid seeing the bars, I put my head between the bars and I could look at the mock orange without any barrier.

The gardener saw me. For a moment, he stayed half hunched over, staring at me. I didn't move. I didn't want to do anything bad. I just wanted to look at the flowers without any barrier, simply, tranquilly, because it was an evening milder than the others.

The gardener bent down, took some dirt, stood up and, turning toward me, molded the dirt in his hands to make a ball out of it, without haste, unhurriedly. Unhurriedly, too, he raised his arm and threw the ball of dirt at the gate, to where my face was. The clod burst on my head and a shower of dirt rained down on me.

When I reopened my eyes, the gardener was molding another clod. I slowly withdrew my head from between the bars and I walked. I didn't run or anything. The clod burst on my back.

At home I washed in a bucket near the old, uncovered cistern. Then I started waiting, sitting against the wall. I listened to the willows chattering in the wind.

38

THE LETTER from Hyères came one evening. It was an official letter, typed, on Air Force letterhead.

I went out and I walked in the evening and the night. In the avenues there were lights, people, the cold that bit faces.

Pierre, when he left, said: "Don't cry, Thumbelina, I'll be back."

I sat down on the steps in front of the station. The chestnut trees raised their oily buds in the sickly light of the streetlamps. I waited until the departure of the Hyères train that Pierre would never take again.

The next morning, I went out very early. A few cars passed by on the gray avenue. Pigeons perched on the dull cobbles of the roadway, flew off with a clapping noise of wings at the approach of cars. One pigeon pecked calmly in the middle of the avenue. It flew off when the car came upon it. The car struck it with its hood. There was a whirl of feathers, the dead pigeon all crumpled on the sidewalk.

It was the early morning of a very gray, very sad Sunday.

39

BACK THEN, in the evenings, as I came back from school, I no longer thought about the mason sitting under the big cedar at the bend. The world was calm. I walked without haste. I knew she would come back late from the mayor's house. I lingered, gathering wild fennel in the ditches, and I carried their anise scent away with me, I peacefully observed the tranquil meadows of the valley, the stiff line of poplars along the river. I walked between the hedges, in little steps, because she wouldn't come home until late. I walked like everyone else, exactly like everyone else, in those happy evenings of returning spring.

I didn't hear his whistling when I came near the cedar, I was walking so quietly I could have fled, turned back, gone through the fields. But no. I didn't hear anything.

Simply, all the sudden, there he was, whistling his little tune, under the cedar that always made the wind cooler. Then, everything stopped, and I stopped. He broke off his whistling and he said: "Good evening, cutie."

While laughing. I stayed there, in the emptiness of the evening. He got up. I jumped over the hedge, I fell, I ran across fields. I ran without looking behind me, I ran and ran and kept running. At last I got to the mayor's farm, where she was still working.

She was pruning the lower branches of the vines. I stopped

not far from her and I called out to her. She raised her head, looked at me, and said: "Go home."

She went back to work. She worked barefoot, mechanically, bent over, without rising from one branch to the next. I waited a moment then I came a little nearer and I again called out, more softly. She didn't answer. I left.

I returned slowly to the house. The wild gladiolas bloomed pink at the edge of the wheat fields.

In the house, I sat in front of the door and did my homework. When I'd finished, I went out to the path, I settled into a hollow in the hedge and I started waiting for her to come back. It was a very long night.

While she washed her feet in the basin of warm water, I sat by the fireplace like when I was little and I said: "I saw Ernest, the mason, under the cedar at the bend."

She continued cleaning the cracks in her heels with a matchstick. I said again: "I saw Ernest, the mason, under the cedar at the bend."

She stood, came right up to me, and gave me a slap on each cheek. She resumed cleaning her feet. I stayed by the fireplace, my cheeks burning, my heart crazy.

40

SHE DIDN'T speak. Sometimes at night she cried. I remember. I said: "Why are you crying?"

She didn't respond. I said: "Don't cry."

I wanted to go to her, to tell her: "Me, you have me."

But she was crying from far, far away. There was, everywhere, a lot of silence, the crazy willows of the river, the barking of the hungry foxes on the hill, and she who cried from far away and who said sometimes: "And me, I've had nothing. Had nothing."

I would have liked to go to her.

41

I MET PIERRE at the station one night because my train had arrived too late, because he had fallen asleep on his train. He had said: “I am Pierre.”

And I: “I am Marie.”

I walked to him in the rutted paths of country roads all the way up to the street that bordered the ocean beneath blooming chestnut trees. He said softly: “Marie. I looked for you, Marie. On the plane I called your name, my lonely one, Marie.”

And I was Marie.

Later he said: “I will take you to the islands of childhood, amid the perfume of frangipani. I will lead you deep into caves where the sea comes to die in the shade of gardens of wild orange trees. We will sleep with the song of the wind in the casuarinas on the hills.”

He said: “Marie. My wife, we will have a child.”

And: “I'm not afraid anymore. A child is life's memory.”

42

IT HAD been a long time that the mayor's wife had been sick, and that, before daybreak, she would leave home to go to their house to work, returning late at night smelling of livestock and cooking. So long that the river willows had lost their silvery cloud of catkins. It had been a long time, too, since the mason had waited under the cedar.

That evening, I was sitting near the door, monitoring the sounds of the gathering night. She would not be home for hours. She only left the fields when it got dark. Me, I waited behind the door, the barking of the foxes raced over the hill, the willows talked in the wind.

I told myself, to measure the time, what she was doing. She was wrapping herself in a long, thick gray apron to milk the cows, she was sitting on the low three-footed stool now, holding the bucket under the cow's udder with her feet, she drew down the milk that foamed in the bucket and sometimes the cow would grow impatient, snort, or give a kick. During this time, the calves suckled with wet noises while butting their heads against their mothers' udders. The dog watched, came to lick up the spilled milk. Maybe, before leaving the barn, she went to see Rose, my calf, who was growing her peaceful horns.

They ate. The children, gangling and hateful with dirty eyes, and the mayor, each in their accustomed place, she in the place of their mother. And me, I waited for her behind the door, listening to the darkness of the night. Maybe, before putting the children to bed, she told them in her monotonous voice the story of the three pretty young girls, Rose, Daisy, and Violet, that slow story where the ogre lies in wait.

She gave the dogs the unusable scraps of the meal, put other scraps in the pail for me. She washed the dishes, dried the dishes, put them away, each thing in its proper place. She swept the kitchen, threw the garbage outside or into the fire. And the mayor, in front of the fire, watched her calmly, and it was like a real family.

And then, she lit the lantern, put out the fire, and left. She traversed the whole night with her swinging lamp; and me behind the door, I waited for the sound of her step and her face at last, her light eyes that looked at nothing.

I was there, in the house, filling the time of waiting for her by telling myself untrue things and true things.

Suddenly I heard the steps. I rose up, with a wild heart. She was coming back early. The mayor's wife was better. They didn't need her anymore. My heart was crazy. I opened the door and I threw myself outside to tell her how long I had waited for her, and how happy I was, happy.

In front of the door, the mason was there. At once, I retreated. I tried to shut the door again, but he had already come in, and anyway, the door had no lock. Barely inside, he said: "Good evening, cutie."

And he began whistling the tune from the big cedar at the bend. I looked for a way to escape, and go hide in the tangle of the crazy willows by the river, and nobody could have found me because nobody, not even the hunters, ever goes there. But it was useless because to get out there was only the door, and he was in front of it.

I thought of her, on the other side of the village, busy milking unknown cows, in an unknown house, with nobody's dog sitting in front of the door. I thought that if she couldn't feel that I was calling her, there was no point in waiting anymore. And it was useless to cry out, the house was so far away below the hill and the trees. So I did nothing, because there was nothing to do.

When he finished whistling, the mason said: "So, cutie, was he good, the priest?"

I said nothing. I began to hope very hard that she would come back at once, that she would open the door, and everything would be in order. But she didn't come back.

The mason pulled the table against the door then he came toward me saying: "You're a proper slut, like her. A slut. You've tried the priest, now you will try the mason, it's better, you'll see."

I said nothing and I let those unbearable things happen because there was nothing to be done, no.

43

As he left, the mason said: "A proper slut, like her."

I went out into the dark and I walked all the way to the river under the willows that shivered in the wind.

I remember the rustling of the wind in the willows, on other nights, and her, asleep on the bench at the police station in her new dress that was all rumpled, the young abbé all in black and all alone.

I walked into the river and I stayed a long time in the icy water that flowed quietly amid the sad song of the willows, and, in the distance, the calls of frogs by the edge of forgotten ponds.

When she came back, I was sitting on the chair by the door. I heard her coming from far away, because of the clomping of Rose, the calf. I said to myself: "She's bringing Rose."

She opened the door and said: "Go get the cow settled."

She carried in a basket full of fresh rye. I pulled Rose toward the shed. She had trouble moving forward because she didn't know the way and it was dark in spite of the lantern. Maybe she didn't want to go in. By tugging on the halter and saying to her, "Come, Rose," I succeeded in tying her to the place I'd set up for her.

I put the grass in front of her and sat beside her with my lantern to give her some light. She began to eat as if she were already getting used to her new home, and from time to time, she raised her head while she ate, or she snorted loudly like all the cows in the world do on all farms. Her strong scent already filled the shed. I said to her: "Soon you will have the duck and the dog with you."

Because I thought that if she were a sociable calf she might miss the presence of her friends, and would like company. Me, I'm not like that, I'm not used to it, but Rose, yes, maybe.

I went back to the house. It was cold everywhere. She had put my dinner on the table and was cleaning her feet, which were perched on the rim of the basin. I began to eat, then I was sick to my stomach and I ran outside to throw up in the grass. I vomited violently and when that was over, I vomited again, and my stomach was seized with cramps. I stayed outside a long time, waiting for things to calm down.

When I came inside, she had put a bowl of steaming linden-blossom tea on the table. I drank it because I was frozen, and immediately I had to run outside. In the end, I went to bed. I was truly very cold.

In the bed, she held me against her to warm me and quickly fell asleep, very far away. I cried because I like crying. I said to myself: "They call her Crazy Genie."

Or: "Everything is unbearable."

I saw again my grandmother in her big armchair between the fireplace and the armoire, and I felt full of hatred.

After crying like that for a while and telling myself about the unbearable things that had happened, I got very hot. I sweated, the sheets were wet. I drew away from her and took off the covers because I was dripping with sweat.

At dawn, she woke up, touched me, and said: "You are sick."

She prepared another bowl of linden-blossom tea and a bran poultice. I fell asleep and after that I was sick for a long time.

44

IT WAS at night that these things happened, always the same ones.

All day long I listened to the wind, near or far, that blew under the roof tiles, trembled in the branches of the river willows, clouded the white sand of the foxes' hill. I looked through the window at the weary branches of the willows swaying or shaking in the wind.

Toward evening, she came home. The heat was rising. The willows, grown enormous, pressed against the windows as if to enter the house. I raised myself in bed, I leaned against the wall that buckled like a soggy cardboard box. The lamp flickered. On the path beside the river, the willows drew the enormous hands of their roots out of the earth. I crawled to get away from them, I wanted to scream. Passersby went by calmly, talked, said: "She is afraid."

And they walked right past me without seeing me. In the village, the dogs left the doorsteps of houses flowering with geraniums, raised their muzzles to the evening sky, and howled into the branches of the willows.

Suddenly, she was there. She rested her light eyes, the color of tears, upon me. I said: "We will go away. We will go far away, to lands where the trees touch the sun, where we will get lost endlessly as we hunt wild cyclamens in the forests of acacias."

She said: “Drink. You are sick.”

I drank the linden blossom tea and I said again: “We will go away. We will go away.”

She stayed sitting in front of the fire. Sometimes, she kept quiet. Sometimes, she began telling, in her vacant voice, the never-ending story of the three young girls, where the beloved ogre turns into a handsome prince.

I fell asleep against her.

45

SHE MADE me infusions of linden blossom, hot milk, very sweet, with eau-de-vie. She prepared inhalations of hay flowers for me, in the cooking pot. She put suction cups on me, applied bran poultices. She dried me off and changed my clothes when I was drenched in sweat. At night, if I was cold, she held me against her to warm me.

I heard her take Rose out in the morning, bring her back at night. When night fell, she stayed in front of the fire, her hands limp, waiting for nothing. Sometimes, while still watching the fire, she told that old story of the three young girls and the ogre. She went very far away. I remember those nights when she told stories for nobody, in front of the fire.

And then, things happened, always the same ones, and there was no way to defend yourself against them, there was only the hope of having the strength to bear them in all those lost evenings.

She was in front of the fire, and I watched her. The floor tiles pleated themselves slowly in front of the bed, the walls of the house drew together, making the bed crack, grasped it ever more tightly. Rubble fell, soon it would cover me. I tried to raise myself, to shout, but my mouth was full of plaster debris. I wanted to push back the walls, they fell apart in dusty fragments. With a superhuman effort, I broke out screaming.

She was there, suddenly, and her light eyes dispelled the ghosts. I said: "Maman. My mother."

And she said: "Shut up."

Then I was cold. She came into the bed, held me against her to warm me. I fell asleep in the milky odor of sweat.

46

AS SOON as I could stand, I went to my grandfather's. My grandmother was doing the washing under the paulownia. I walked around the house to keep far away from her, and I went inside. My grandfather was reading in his old books of yesteryear. I said: "Grandfather."

He raised his head and said: "It's you, little one."

And at once he fumbled with his only hand in the musette bag that he always wore and gave me a yellow apple. He said: "These are St. John apples. Eat, Marie."

I started eating and he resumed reading. I waited a moment for him to remember and then I said: "I've come for the puppy. I'm going to call him Ash, for the tree that shakes in the wind."

Then he explained that it was too late. I should have come long before, the grandmother had given away the puppy.

I said to him, to excuse myself: "I've been sick."

He looked at me then stood up. He came back with a bottle that was all dusty: "Drink a glass of this once a day. It's a very old wine. It will do you good. You are quite thin, little one."

After a moment, he added: "She, too, she was thin. You look like her. But she, she was always cheerful. She sang from morning till night. Afterward there was that great misfortune."

I left with my bottle. As I passed near the grandmother's well, I threw in the apple core. I went down the meadow at a gallop toward the damp willow trees of the river. As I passed by the cistern in the ground by the hedge, I leaned over and threw in the bottle of old wine. I went to see Rose, who was tethered to a bush near there, and who was quietly eating. I said to her: "You won't have a puppy. The grandmother gave it away. She did it on purpose. She's a pest. But I will bring you a duck. His name will be Benoît."

Rose looked happy.

I sat near her and waited for her to come back. It was that night that I perceived that Rose was blind. I stayed near her talking about Benoît, about the puppy we would have one day and who would guide her, and about her, who used to laugh all the time, in the past, when I wasn't born yet. Rose quietly ruminated. She was pretty, with her white spots on her black coat, and her stubborn horns, and no doubt she didn't know that other animals could see.

When she came back I went out to welcome her. After dinner, while she was cleaning her feet in the basin, I said to her: "Rose is blind."

After a moment, she said: "We'll have to be careful at the cistern."

I had trouble falling asleep. I thought about the calf, about the sunken cistern with no cover. I couldn't stop thinking of unbearable things, and of her bleary, blind eyes.

47

THE LETTER came from Hyères. I understood before even opening it. It was an official letter, typed, written by nobody. It said: "Pierre died honorably and will be buried with all the honors due him," and I could attend the burial if I liked, and they told me what day and where he would be interred with all those honors.

I walked in the streets and arrived at the station where I had waited, sitting on the steps, for the train to Hyères to depart. It was cold on the steps and the chestnut trees raised their big syrupy buds. When I accompanied him to the station, Pierre said, "Don't feel bad, Thumbelina. I'll be back."

He held me against him: "I will take you to gentle, fragrant islands of blue shade and sunshine."

He spoke of the white stars of the frangipani, the giant spiders that weave giant webs between the trees, the birds of paradise in the deep caves.

"I will take you far away and we will sleep in the garden of grapefruits, in the murmur of the casuarina trees."

When he took me on the plane, he said: "You are my earth. The earth is beautiful. We will ride horseback on a shooting star."

And when he left: "Thumbelina. My earth. My wife. Don't cry. I'll be back."

I took the train to Hyères and they buried him.

There was military music and military salutes, there were speeches full of words, he was their best test pilot, wreaths full of ribbons and words, me and the orange marigolds, a little old woman all in black and Pierre in front, all alone in his coffin. I wasn't permitted to look at him. And then, Pierre wouldn't have wanted me to see him dead, torn to pieces. He said: "I'm not afraid anymore, my sweet. We will have a child. A child is life's memory."

But there would be no child.

48

AFTER the departure of the military men and the priest, the cemetery became sunlit silence. I stayed for a while sitting on the pile of earth near Pierre. The little old woman in black was crying. I thought of Pierre who said: "We will have a child. A child is life's memory."

Or, on the platform at the station: "My wife. My earth. Don't feel bad. I'll be back."

I went to see the other graves, neatly arranged in their rows, with their headstones decorated with crosses, their wreaths of pearls, their flower arrangements. I read the names of the dead, their ages, looked at photos of children dead for eternity. Then I wanted to see Pierre again, but the gravediggers were there. I left.

The little old woman in black was waiting at the cemetery gate, her purse on her arm, her old hands placed one on top of the other. She came up to me and said: "You are Marie."

I said: "Yes."

Then she said: "Me, I'm his aunt. He told you about me. I raised him from when he was very little."

I said: "Yes."

And we walked without saying anything, in the sunshine and under the trees, in front of the railings of gardens where the orange trees were dropping their petals. We arrived at the sea and sat down listening to its noise and to the breath of the wind in the pines.

49

We stayed a long time under the pines, facing the sea. Clusters of seagulls played in the silky sky. The little old woman in black cried noiselessly and her wrinkled cheeks were glazed with tears. I could have held out my hand, stroked her tearstained face. She stayed that way, thinking her own thoughts, and then she said: "He always talked about you. He said you came from the islands. When he was little, he wanted to be an explorer of islands. But that doesn't exist, so then he wanted to become an airplane pilot. I couldn't stop him. I was always waiting for the day when he would have the accident. Now it has come, he has gone to join the others. He has told you that."

For a moment I said nothing. Then I reflected and I said: "No. He said he didn't want to talk about the past."

She explained that he never spoke about it because he didn't want to remember: "When, at the age of four, you've seen your father and mother die because of the war, you don't want to talk about it." As for me, she said, I could speak calmly, with all those sunny isles where I'd spent my childhood. But him. When he decided to be an aviator, she'd thought it was so he could see the islands and die afterward like his father and his mother.

The little old woman in black fell silent. She choked up. The sound of the sea rose, the hoarse calls of the gulls on the water and in the sky. The wind carried the scent of seaweed and pines to the city.

The little old woman wanted to know about the islands. I continued watching the movement of the froth of the waves, hearing Pierre's voice telling of the perfume of the frangipani, the deep caves where the red birds nest, the gardens of wild orange trees, the blue sand of gentle beaches, and the water of the night, the lonely cry of the herons. I thought of the crazy willows of the river, of the big paulownia that rocked the sky with its mauve clusters, and of her, the one they called Crazy Genie because she didn't talk and because she had had me, whom nobody wanted.

Then I told the little old woman in black the things Pierre would say, and also about the cries of the jackals, the night on the edge of the deserts, the transparent green waters, lost atolls in the ocean, the silence of afternoons crushed by sunshine, and the mangroves whose roots rise from the earth like giant houses that climb to the sky. And then, too, those lost islands where the wind is so savage that nothing can live there, ever.

The little old woman listened and said, after a long while: "When you've known things like those, you can speak of them without doing harm to anybody."

Then she talked about Pierre.

50

EVERY night when I came home from school, I untied the calf from her tree or her stake and led her along the path or to the edge of the fields so she could graze on the new grass. I talked to her about my own concerns.

I told her about her, of what the grandfather had told me, that before she had me she would laugh and sing day and night, and that later, once she was expecting me, she never wanted to say who my father was, and the grandmother, who is a bad woman, had gone into a fury because she didn't want things like that to happen in her family, which was the most respectable in the village. Then she had moved into the shack under the crazy willows that talk at night, and she had never gone back to her home, and she worked at people's houses to be fed, and they called her Crazy Genie because she never talked, but she wasn't crazy, she simply didn't talk and didn't laugh.

I told these things to Rose, and I was happy because I could talk to her calmly, without fear. She was a true friend. To console her for being blind, I told her what some of the girls at my school were like. There's one who has, on one hand, four fingers fused, two by two, and on the other, three normal fingers and a forked thumb, which is inconvenient for writing. There's one who has one foot that turns in and she runs poorly, dragging her foot, and if she wasn't so mean, she would be pitied; and her brother who has white hair and red eyes; and another boy whose knees turn out and he walks with his legs herky-jerky and it's embarrassing to see him, luckily, he's at the boys' school.

Rose listened while quietly eating. From time to time she flicked her velvety ears or snorted hard as if to take part in the conversation, or shook her tail with a contented air.

I taught her to be guided by voice. I would stand in front of her, on her left, and say: "Come, Rose."

And I pulled her toward my voice. I did the same thing on the right. I made her walk fast, then I said: "Slowly, Rose."

Or: "Stop, Rose."

And I taught her to slow down or to stop.

She understood very quickly because she was a smart calf. She listened to all the sounds and recognized them. She knew to move away from the noise of the river and the willows that were crazy in the wind. I took her on a tour of the area so she wouldn't be afraid and so she would know how to get around on her own, and soon she knew. From that moment on, I was less sad that she was blind, and she was, too.

When night fell and the time came when she could come home, I went to meet her with Rose. I sat against the hedge. Rose stayed there, calm, waiting with me, or grazed a little more in the grass and the leaves, to treat herself. I waited. Time slowed. I tried again to talk to Rose but I couldn't anymore. Finally I heard her step before I could even make out her shadow. I stood up. I would have liked to run to her. When she got near me, she said: "Go back to the house."

All three of us walked to the house, her in front, then me, then Rose, on the nighttime path.

Along the river, the willows answered the wind. She walked on with her blank face.

51

THE LITTLE old woman in black sits facing the sea and remembers. She lets her old hands rest limply on her stomach. Every so often she chokes up. She says: "We lived far away, in the mountains. On winter nights, we slept in the barns, near the cows, for warmth. When it got so cold that the wild animals were dying of hunger, we put the chickens in the kitchen so they wouldn't be devoured. The foxes sniffed the scent and came to howl beneath the windows. We stayed in bed listening to the howling and had goosebumps because we understood how hungry they were."

She says: "In the spring, the boys went up very high in the mountains to bring edelweiss to the girls. We heard them singing in the distance, by the peaks, and we were a little afraid that they wouldn't come back."

She says all the young people dreamed of going to Brazil. They spoke of those countries where people ate meat with every meal without fear, and there was so much of it that they didn't know what to do with it. All the young people dreamed of going over there. Their trips were paid for. The ones who left never came back and they never even wrote.

The little old woman talks of the springtimes of her childhood. She tells of the sound of the silkworms that devour the leaves of the mulberry trees in their racks. They would buy the eggs. They would put them in the children's beds and the children would lie down on them to keep the eggs warm until the worms were born. All the children of the village hatched silkworms, and the streets were silent.

Once the worms were born, they put them in stacked drying racks, and then all the children roosted in the mulberry trees to gather the leaves, and if the leaves were wet they had to be dried or the worms would die, and that was a great misfortune. The worms ate and ate, and the whole house lived to the rhythm of their hungry crunching, day and night. Sometimes, all was quiet: The worms were sleeping. She reflects for a moment and says: "They were as pretty as children."

Some days, the racks had to be cleaned. They would remove all the worms, clean up, carpet the racks with fresh newspapers, put the worms back in, and everything would start over, the noise of the jaws, night and day, cut by the silence of the rest periods.

Then, when the worms had eaten enough, they put out branches for them. The worms would choose their positions and start closing themselves up in their silk cocoons. There was nothing left to do but wait for them to fall completely asleep to boil the cocoons. Then the merchants would come. The little old woman says: "We were little, we worked and we were happy. We were happy with the bright green mulberry trees, with the noise the silkworms made while they ate, and when they slept there was an emptiness as if someone had gone. We were happy with the nights in the barns, and the neighbors coming. The men talked in low voices about politics, the women knitted or mended. Yes. We were happy. When Pierre was born, it already wasn't like that anymore. We were too poor. And then, there was the war. Afterward, the little one was never the same."

She stopped talking. The sound of the sea mounted, the cool breeze in the pines, the cries of the gulls. She recalls: "I still hear the voice of little Pierre. At night, I still wake up. I hear him saying: Cover my ears, Auntie, cover my ears. We were running on the roads and the planes were bombing, he, he would say: Cover my ears, Auntie. At night I hear him. After all that, he was never the same. When you've seen your mother hanged, your father dead in a stream, and when you've run under bombardment, you don't feel like talking and laughing anymore. For you, it's not the same. You were in the islands."

I say nothing. I think of her, whom they called Crazy Genie, never otherwise. The little old woman cries softly, her hands limp, facing the sea.

"When he was little, he went to the circus, one time. It was the first circus, right after the war. After that, he wanted to be a clown. I said: That's not a trade. And it's true that it's not a trade. But he, he wanted to be a clown. He said he would go far, far away, in a trailer, with a horse, all alone, and he would make children laugh. He would pretend to be a clown. I see him as if he were here. He would put on his grandfather's clothes, the hat, and he would stay in the courtyard, arms crossed. I went looking for him. He said: I am the scarecrow for the sparrows. And me, it made me cry to see the ideas he had. And then, he died. Everyone is dead."

52

In springtime, I sometimes went to the farms on Thursdays. I cut the thistles in the wheat that had resisted the weedkillers. I ran through the fields, barefoot, with a stick topped with a blade at one end, and I cut down the thistles. The wheat gleamed in the sunshine and the sun made your head spin.

At other times, like the hatching season for chicks, ducklings, goslings, and turkey poults, I had to chase away birds of prey. The buzzard or the sparrow hawk or the kite rose from the woods, glided in the sky above the brood. The mothers went crazy, called their little ones with great squawking. The little ones ran for refuge under the mothers' open wings. Me, I had to shout very loud so the bird would get scared and go away. But sometimes it would stay there, despite my cries, immobile in the sky, then suddenly drop to earth and take off again in full flight toward the woods, its prey squeaking between its claws.

At noon, I ate at the farm. The people talked. I helped do the dishes, swept the kitchen while the people drank coffee.

Before going back to work, if she was working not far from there, I would go to the edge of the fields to try to spot her. The fields were empty. I would wait a moment, then go look at other fields. Finally, I would leave. All afternoon, I would wait for night to come, to go home, for her to come back.

Sometimes she was in the fields, bent over the dirt. My heart would seize up, I would run to her across the land. I would stop near her, I would call to her softly. Sometimes she kept working. Sometimes she straightened up, looked at me, and said in her bleak voice: "Go work."

Then she would bend down again to the dirt. I would wait a bit, but I knew very well that she didn't want me to be there. I would set out slowly again across the fields.

Once again, I watched for birds of prey, I cut the thistles in the sun, I waited for the night to come, for her to arrive on the path with her basket, for her to eat in silence, for her to clean the cracks in her heels in silence, for her to go to bed and, perhaps, hold me against her.

At last evening came. I went home at a run. I waited on the path for her return, sitting under the sweetbriar with the drooping branches. As soon as I heard her footstep I stood up, with a crazy heart. When she came near me, she said: "Go back to the house."

And I went home behind her, with Rose.

I always wanted to tell her that I was there waiting for her, that I was so happy, so happy that she had come back this night again, that me, I loved her. But her face was full of silence.

53

IN THE summertime, the uncles, aunts, and cousins came to spend their vacation in the grandmother's big house. The screams and the laughter erupted from the hillside, scattered across the valley all the way to the darkest of the willows, climbed up the foxes' white hill where I went sometimes to wander. The lounge chairs were strewn outside my grandmother's house, under the oak, under the big paulownia that had long since shed its petals. The girl cousins sunbathed, lying on the grass in the meadows. I climbed up the hill and watched them.

Sometimes—back before the time of the abbé all alone in his black cassock; before the policemen and the journalists who asked questions to which I said: "No. No." Before the mason under the cedar at the bend and inside the house—I would go in summertime to the grandmother's house. As soon as I opened the door, the laughing faces would turn toward me, recognize me, fall silent. I would settle in beside the grandfather, who was always reading, in old books spotted with damp, the history of distant kings who'd died of great folly, or the history of the men of hell, of that unfortunate one who burned eternally for having devoured his children.

I would say: "Grandfather."

He would slowly raise his eyes from his book, saying: "It's you, little one."

He would give me some walnuts, some hazelnuts, or an apple and say: "Eat, little one."

I remember that, the silence, and the grandmother who said to the others: "She's come to spy on us."

And me, I was little.

I would leave. The door barely shut, the laughter and the voices would fill the house, like music. I would eat the apple behind the house, near the well, or break the hazelnuts or the walnuts with a rock on the edge, I would throw the apple core or the shells into the grandmother's well. I would hurtle across the great meadow at a run toward the willows that spoke to the wind.

When I got home, if she was there, she would say: "I don't want you going up there."

At the end of days of great heat, when the air cooled a little, the uncles, aunts, and cousins sometimes walked down the big meadow to the river with baskets and folding chairs. They would settle at the edge of the water, swim, eat, laugh, and all the river, the willows, and, higher up, the poplars resonated with those sounds.

She seemed to hear nothing, kept working away with empty eyes, far from everything.

Some nights, the boy cousins and girl cousins walked by our house, as if they didn't see it. On those nights, I climbed up the foxes' hill, I sat in the brush and I played with the white sand, or by a fox hole, and then I told myself the story of a fox who would leave his den if I waited long enough, and I would tame him, he would follow me everywhere. But I knew it wasn't true, because foxes have many exits to their dens. I hunted crows' nests, I told myself that I would tame them, too, I would teach them to speak, to stay perched on my shoulders or on my head, and everyone, the foxes, the crows, and me, we would love one another peaceably, like happy families.

When the aunts, uncles, boy cousins, and girl cousins went back with their baskets and folding chairs, I ran to the house and I went to her, my heart crazy with sadness and joy. I stopped right up close to her. She was working, always the same, and on seeing her, I thought that nothing had come to disturb the water that flowed gently, nor the voice of the willows in the wind.

54

ROSE, MY calf, was getting more and more beautiful, and her hide shone in the sun, was soft to the touch. She recognized voices, raised her head, and came near as soon as I called her. She had known for a long time how to guide herself. Nobody could have known, when she walked behind me, calmly and assuredly like the happy little cow she was, that she could not see. She forgot about it, and me too, I forgot about it, it's true. We were so happy, the two of us, that we had no time to think of sad things.

It was at the end of spring that I brought back the duck Benoît. One Thursday, as I left a farm where I'd weeded corn all day and my back hurt a lot, I came across a lost duckling who was calling for his mother. I picked him up and at once he calmed down, happy. Then I thought of Rose all alone outside the old house, whom I'd promised to bring a little duck. I left the farm with Benoît in my arms, without even turning around to see if anyone had seen me. Nobody said anything to me, ever.

When I got home, I went at once to show Benoît to Rose. Rose looked happy and Benoît began to chatter.

At nightfall, when the time came when she might return, I went out into the path to meet her with Rose on a halter and Benoît in my arms. I sat down under the sweetbriar, and I waited. Benoît wanted to run away, I held on to him, because

I thought it would take him a while to get used to things. I had explained to him, and I had promised him, that later, when he had gotten used to his new home, I would take him to the river, to the streams, and to the ponds full of frogs and crazy reeds. I had told him that he would sleep in a crate lined with straw, near Rose, and that when he was big, he would lay eggs wherever he liked. He listened, his head bent down, and then, as soon as I stopped talking, he started crying again to call for his mother and that made me sad, on this path, under the sweetbriar, with the night that was falling, and she who wasn't coming home.

Finally, I heard her steps, I stood up in the path with Benoît who wouldn't stop crying. When she was near me, I said: "I brought back a little duck to keep Rose company."

But she could see that well enough. She kept walking and I saw how tired she was because she too had stayed in the cornfields working nonstop. When we got home, Benoît was still peeping. She said: "He's hungry."

And she made him chopped salad with crushed hard-boiled eggs. Benoît ate well.

I was as happy as can be, and I started talking a lot. I told her how happy the calf and the duck would be. The duck would paddle in the river, Rose would eat grass, and me, I would watch them among the willows. And then one day, Rose would have little calves, Benoît would hatch his eggs, and the house would be full of animals, and everyone would be happy.

She said nothing and I could see how tired she was from working all day in the cornfields. She went to sleep immediately, and me, I didn't stop imagining all the animals we would have in the house, the cheerful noise that would make and, sometimes, we would probably have to get angry to make them quiet down. I thought of her with her bleak eyes, and I really would have liked to wake her up so I could keep talking to her about all these animals, so she could hold me against her a little like she sometimes did and I could sleep at last.

The next night she brought back some ground corn and rye in her basket for Benoît. I went up to her to talk to her, but her eyes were distant, and she said as usual: "Go back to the house."

I went home with Benoît and Rose.

55

OFTEN, I remember the days and nights I spent with Rose, my calf, and the duck Benoît.

Benoît had gotten quite used to the house, to Rose, to me, and to her. He followed us everywhere, because he was a duck who liked company, exactly like some people, but not me. He ate grass, seeds from the meadows and the hedges, bugs, and, at night, corn or rye. When he was full, or, now and then, between two beakfuls, he chattered with a contented air. He really liked to chatter like that. And me, I was happy. He grew in front of my eyes, and his youthful down got covered, on his back, wings, and tail, with stiff and shining feathers that he liked to fluff out and smooth in turn. I led him to the river, I led him to the ponds edged with reeds and crazy rushes, and Benoît played in the water while Rose quietly grazed, and me, I watched, calm, while tearing up leaves of wild mint.

Yes. Those were lovely days.

Sometimes, I glimpsed between the trees the grandmother's white house, up on the hill, which watched us, with its black cypress that reached up to the heavens, its vast curly oak, and the big paulownia under which I no longer went to lie down.

At night, we went up the path to meet her. I sat beneath the hedge and watched the path in the dusk to look for her shadow. Trying to quit waiting and make the time go faster, I told stories to Rose and Benoît. I told the story of the beautiful princesses who climb castle towers so tall that they stop the clouds, towers where the nights are thickened with cries, where the days fill the shadows of the roads with dust, of days in the desert where those who are being awaited arrive too late. Especially I told the story of Penelope, who wears out her eyes in dark caverns; and of Lorelei, who climbs the highest rocks and reaches into the tumultuous waters of the Rhine; of Ophelia, lover of water lilies, who escapes, lying down on the milky water of the rivers, and nothing is left but the wake of her golden hair.

I told stories, and if I didn't know more, I made things up, and nonetheless, I waited for her to return. I was afraid she would abandon us there, alone on this path with night everywhere.

At last, she approached. I rose up toward her. She came near me with her basket on her arm and said: "So then, go back home."

56

ABRUPTLY, that summer, the rains stopped, as if they'd vanished. The crops withered, the trees turned gray with thirst, and the earth opened up in wide cracks, gaping at the sky. All that remained of the river was the rocky bed, cluttered with old bottles and other trash that people had thrown there, back when there was water. Dogs roamed the riverbed searching for any trickle.

She barely worked anymore. The men had withdrawn into the darkest parts of their houses and only came out to interrogate the white sky that threw its cement heat on the earth.

When, at every meal, we ate jam, I understood that our provisions were exhausted. She stayed in front of the house, sitting, her hands clasped, looking at nothing.

I took water from the cistern for Benoît and for Rose. One day she said: "The cistern is almost dry."

Then I began wandering from pond to pond, Benoît thirsty in my arms, looking for water. I left Rose outside the house to graze on the scanty grass. The ponds, long since dried up, showed nothing but a bottom of cracked ancient mud, on the surface of which frogs had come to shrivel under the demented sun. The fields were gray and gritty.

At home, there was less and less water in the cistern. She filtered it into the jug with a handkerchief. One day she said, looking at the duck who had become drab and was losing his feathers: "He will die."

I thought for a long time. When night came, at the time when people gather around tables, I took Benoît in my arms and went to a farm that was supplied by the village water tower. I put Benoît in the farmyard near a tractor tire that was open and filled with water. At once, he drank then got into the water and began frolicking with joy. I went home.

Another day, she said: "We've got nothing left to eat. We have to sell Rose."

At once my heart went crazy and it was as if the earth and the house and the trees were spinning. When I had calmed down a little, I said: "But it will rain soon."

She said nothing for a moment then replied: "Even if it rains, it's too late."

Once again the world started spinning like a crazy top. I said: "She is blind. Nobody will want her."

She said: "At the Borderie, they'll take her."

I thought of all the cows at the Borderie, of the dogs ceaselessly barking with all their foaming teeth bared. I said: "She is blind. She won't understand what is happening. She won't be able to understand and to defend herself, blind and all, the way she is."

She said nothing more and I knew very well that it wasn't her fault, this weather, the crazy sky, the crazy sun, and all the scorched crops in the fields, the trees burned by the heat and the earth open in wide cracks, the dried-up frogs on the surface of the ponds and in the reddish rushes, faces up to the white sky. I thought of Rose, alone in the middle of all those strange cows who would attack her and she wouldn't know how to defend herself because she couldn't see; Rose, chased by those wild dogs and not knowing where to go to seek refuge.

That night when she lay down to sleep, I lay down against her. I put my head in the hollow of her neck, and I cried over Rose because there was nothing to do or to understand. She said: "There's nothing else we can do."

But me, I cried into her neck, I could no longer stop myself. She fell asleep.

The next day she took Rose to the Borderie.

57

THE DAYS and nights began with neither Rose nor Benoît. She stayed in front of the house, her hands clasped, looking at nothing, straight ahead.

Sometimes, while she remained facing the silent willows of the dried-up river, I went wandering on the outskirts of the Borderie to try and spot Rose. I watched from afar the herds of cows with the dogs in fields that were gray with thirst and then I went away. I didn't know if Rose was still there.

Other times I went up the foxes' hill. The white sand burned the feet. On the bushes, nothing was left but spines. I searched for signs of life from the wild rabbits, foxes, crows, and magpies. There was nothing but the pale sand, the naked bushes, and the white and silent heat of the earth and sky.

I saw at the summit of the other hill the grandmother's big house, which seemed to watch me with its black cypress pointed at the white sky. I would have liked to go under the paulownia to see if it was dying of thirst. It was the time when the aunts and the girl cousins from town came for their vacation. If I were to go into the house, they would keep silent and in this silence the grandmother would say: "She has come to spy on us."

Sometimes, too, I followed the course of the river, looking for water. But there was no water anywhere. I looked at the rubbish people had thrown away. I poked at it with a stick, for no reason, to see.

When I went home, she was still there, in front of the house, her hands hanging limply, or, if it was dinnertime, in the kitchen making food.

One morning she left with the bucket to the farms that were supplied by the water tower. She came back with clean water. From that day on, every morning she went from farm to farm with her bucket, but they gave her little because the water was rationed. We washed the clothes in the dirty water of the cistern.

Our faces and eyes were as gray as the thirsty earth.

58

ONE NIGHT, the storm came. The thunder, which exploded at ground level, terrified the region. The rains streamed in rivers across the overdried land.

We watched the water falling from the doorway and then I went outside and danced in the rain while singing at ear-splitting volume. And then, the water came into the house and we had to put barriers in front of the door, then clean off the mud that had entered the kitchen. We were happy to work and to see the water. Her face had returned to normal.

Two days later, the water began to flow in the river, the willows to talk in the wind.

Once again she went to people's houses to prepare the soil, sow the green beans, weed the green beans, water them, and life began again as before. Sometimes, I went with her. At night, she brought back in her basket potatoes, jars of preserves, sometimes an old, tired hen, sometimes old clothes. Everything like before.

I waited for her the same way on the path. When she was late, I didn't know if she would come back after all those days of hunger and thirst. She finally came back.

One night I said: "We could get Rose and Benoît back."

She said: "We don't have enough money anymore."

I understood that Rose was lost forever.

59

AT HARVEST time, things seemed to be returning to the way they were before the drought.

Every day, she left in the dew-silvered dawn with her basket. As she left, she said: "Keep sleeping."

But I got up. I ate my bowl of bread and café au lait, imitating her gestures, I swept the kitchen and pushed the rubbish far from the door, I put the dishes away in the big armoire.

I left the house early. I took detours across fields to see her in the vineyards. Most often she was alone there at that hour. She was squatting beneath the vines. Sorrow washed over me. I wanted to go to her and tell her I loved her. But she would have said: "Get out of here."

I just watched, and then I took the path to school between hedges that were damp with dew.

At night, I joined her in the vineyards. The harvesters talked and laughed above the vine rows in the sugary odor of must, the buzzing of bees around the vats. She worked ceaselessly.

Sometimes they sent her into the cornfields to cut the corn tops for the cows. The corn was puny and dried out that year. She cut off the tops, made them into piles, and I helped her carry the piles to the edge of the fields. Our hair was full of corn-tassel debris and our hands were black with corn smut. After a while, she said: "Go home."

I stayed a little longer. Then I went back to the house. I sat on the ground in front of the door, like her in the time of the drought, and I did my homework. When I was done, I went out onto the path, toward her, who would return at the edge of night. I sat under the sweetbriar bushes that were empty of flowers. I listened to the willows in the wind. I waited in the night for her to come back, her shadow, her weary step. The talkative willow branches were in a panic.

On Thursdays I could go with her to the grape harvesting. Those were happy days. The autumn grew sweet; sweet was the buzzing of the bees around the vats, the smell of the fermenting grapes; sweet was the laughter of the men and women in the vineyards. The children played. I stayed near her. We refilled the baskets that the men emptied into the sacks and sometimes they said: "How's it going, Crazy Genie?"

At lunch, we ate in the sheds. We ate without fear, to fullness. She kept quiet and the people talked loudly. We returned to harvesting, leaving behind us the devastated rows from where, already, torn leaves were disappearing. She worked in silence and sometimes someone said to her: "So, Crazy Genie, how's it going?"

And she worked, and me, I was happy.

When night came, we went into the corn to cut off the tops of the plants. I took the tops to the edge of the fields and later the men came to pick them up with the tractor. She was there, her hair mixed with corn-tassel debris, her hands blackened with corn smut. I looked at her and wanted to tell her how happy I was that the two of us were there working quietly in the cornfield, far from the others.

The swallows covered the electric wires, I recall. The chestnut trees were losing their shiny chestnuts. I went under the hazelnut trees and ate hazelnuts, under the walnut trees and ate walnuts. If there were a lot of them, I put them in her basket and we stored them in the attic for winter. The figs were lovely. The farmers gave us some.

We stayed to eat. She helped to milk the cows, to empty the small vats into bigger vats. I waited not far from her in the semidarkness filled with darting bats.

We went home. She had in her basket some figs, some plums that she would dry in the sun in racks on the roof of the house, grapes that she would hang from strings attached to the ceiling, sometimes some grape must that she would turn into jam, apples that she would put in the attic and which smelled good all winter. At night, the house smelled of sugar. Caramelized scents pooled in the corners, in the armoire, under the fireplace, floated around the house and out to the edge of the river amid the incessant rustling of the willows.

60

THERE was the Thursday when we went to Antoine's to harvest the grapes. I didn't mark this day more than the others at the time, because nothing ever warns us when we're in the process of experiencing a special day, a beginning and an ending, even when it's a happy beginning, because certain things appear normal or happy, and afterward you see that they become terrible.

What I know is that she did not work in the vine rows that day, but in the kitchen.

Antoine's sister had just died and he no longer had anyone for the house.

I also remember the swallows on the wires, the thick morning fog that made the willows cottony, the sunrise, the drops of dew on the spiderwebs of the night. I remember those things because I loved them. There was, also, the big herd of cows at the Borderie locked behind their electrified fence and among them, maybe, Rose, but how to know. She, she walked ahead as always, with her wooden basket and her jute bag and me, behind, I almost had to run to keep up with her.

Antoine was waiting for us. In the farmyard of his house, the tractor and its trailer loaded with the vat and baskets awaiting the harvesters. Antoine told her what to make for dinner and at once we went into the fields to pick vegetables and we shelled the white beans to make beans with mutton. We worked and we were fine, both of us, and Antoine was nice. He was there in the kitchen talking while he waited for the others.

At night, after supper, the dishes done, the vats emptied, the wine drunk, he filled several wine bottles and he said: "That's for you, Genie."

And he wanted to take us home in his car. She said: "No."

Because nobody ever took us home and cars never came to our house. But he insisted. He said it wasn't an ordinary night and finally we sat in the car and he took us home.

He talked a lot with a lot of gestures. On the road that led to our place, he said that really it was no place to live, our house, with all those willows everywhere and that hill full of scrub brush and hungry foxes and sand that couldn't even be used to make houses. She said nothing and I could sense all the exhaustion she was feeling.

Antoine came into the house with his bottles of wine. He looked all around him, the old armoire, the old bed, the table with rocks under its legs because the legs were worn away from age. He said: "This is not a house to live in."

And then: "Bring out the glasses, Genie. We will have a drink."

And that's when, while he was drinking, he asked her to come live with him. He said he'd been thinking about it for a long time, that he had hesitated because people called her Crazy Genie, but he knew well that she was not crazy and everyone knew it, that, in any case, she came from the best family in the village, that she was as brave as a man, and as for cooking, she did not have her equal in the whole countryside, and as for him, that was what he cared about. The rest, what everyone called her and all that, didn't matter.

She stayed a moment not speaking, and I felt all her exhaustion, and me, I wanted her to say, No, and for him to leave. In the end, she said: "And the little one?"

He said: "I've thought about that. Soon, she will have finished school. She will go to work."

Then she said immediately: "She will continue with school. She's a good student, she will get an education."

He said that was difficult because he did not have a lot of land, and it would be good if I brought money to the household quickly. She began to wash the glasses, to wipe them and to put them away. Once more, she said: "The little one will go to school."

Antoine left, telling her to reconsider, because what she was asking was difficult, that, truly, it was no life, to live in a crumbling house, under thickets of willows, by the side of a hill full of rabid foxes, crows, and bad animals that nobody knew.

Silence fell. The voice of the willows sounded nearby. She busied herself for a while by cleaning her heels with a matchstick. Hardly had she lain down in bed when she fell asleep, very far off. I listened to her heavy breathing, the hot, milky odor of her sweat. I tried to imagine the two of us in Antoine's house and all the world's despair overcame me. I wanted to wake her, to tell her to stay with me in the old house, to stay always with me in the house, that me, I loved the talking willows, the foxes, and the crows of the hill of white sand, and the big paulownia in front of the grandmother's house. But she slept so far away, at the bottom of all those years of exhaustion.

To soothe myself, I tried to imagine that I would go to school, that I would learn all the things I wanted to know about everything. I would have money. I would come back to get her at Antoine's house and take her very far from there, to countries of sea and eternal sunshine where you laugh all day long, countries where the vines climb up to the sky, where you endlessly get lost in forests of acacias, in search of the scent of wild cyclamens. One day, much later, we would come back to the old house that smelled of jam and we would laugh about the crazy voices of the willows in the wind.

To soothe myself, I told her, in my mind: "I will go study by the sea."

And I chose La Rochelle because of the ocean and because of a photo I'd seen, the Siege of La Rochelle, a long time ago. Immediately, I wanted to wake her to tell her to stay with me in the old house, always with me, and I cried because she was sleeping so far away in her exhaustion.

61

I WAS WOKEN with a jolt by thunder. The shutters at the door, which she never closed, banged against the walls. The willows whistled in the wind. I shook her and I told her: "There's a storm."

She said: "It's nothing. Sleep."

But I couldn't anymore. I listened to the roar of the storm. And all of a sudden I heard barking, distant, then closer. I was very afraid. I shook her again and I said: "There's a whole lot of dogs outside the house."

And I thought of the wild foxes and the animals Antoine talked about, beasts nobody even knew the names of. I repeated: "There's a whole lot of wild dogs outside the house."

She said again: "It's nothing."

But the furious barking came nearer and we got up. The thunderclaps and the noise of the dogs mingled with the gushing of the downpour and the terror of the willows. Suddenly I thought of Rose. Suddenly it seemed to me that it was her the dogs were chasing. Without knowing it, I'd always thought the dogs would chase her like that, because she didn't look like normal cows. I said: "It's Rose coming back."

And just then we heard galloping. I said: "She's going to fall into the cistern."

Immediately I went out and ran toward the cistern. Rose

got there before me. She couldn't see it. There was a sound of sliding rocks, a thud of water and crazy mooing, crazed mooing calls, amid the fury of the dogs. Me, I began to scream and scream. She got there and said: "Stay there. I'm going to the Borderie."

And she left at a run.

I chased off the dogs with blows from old rocks from the well. I stayed near Rose. She still called out, but weakly. Then, to give her patience, I began to talk to her. I told her everything that had happened since her departure, the hunger and the thirst, the dead frogs dried up in the ponds, torn apart facing the crazy sky, Benoît, his beak open with thirst, and her, her sitting with her hands clasped in front of the house, her empty eyes fixed on the distance, and then Antoine, who wanted her to go live with him and the sea that I had never seen, the sun that burns everything in certain lands and even faces, and then the wild cyclamens that you chase until you get lost in the forests of acacias, and the vines that climb to the sky.

During this time, the rain fell hard on the ground, the water channels gushed gurgling into the well and I told Rose that she had gone to look for help and that she was going to rescue her, she could do anything, that she should be patient just a little longer. I said: "Wait a little, Rose."

And Rose mooed again a little. I told her about other things and the time passed and I said again: "Wait a little longer, Rose."

And Rose went quiet. I was afraid and I continued to tell her how much I loved her, how happy I was that she had escaped and come back to us, that she would stay always now, that me, I would work and I would get myself paid so I could buy her back. And when I had finished, I told her the things again so she would be patient and the rain quieted down.

The men arrived a long time afterward with a hoist to pull Rose out of the well. They lit up the cistern and said: "She's dead."

I went into the house and I waited for morning while talking to Rose, my blind calf, who had wanted to come back to us and who was dead.

62

AFTER the night when Antoine took us home in his car, everyone wanted to take us home by car. It was always the same thing. They said: "Come on, Crazy Genie. We'll take you home."

She said at once: "No. No. I prefer to go on foot."

But the people thought it wasn't true, that she would rather go by car like they did, that she said no so as not to inconvenience them. Yet it was true that she preferred to go home alone, and me too, I preferred it. But nobody wanted to believe it. They said, with voices full of patience: "Come on, Crazy Genie, go along with it. Because we're offering."

She said: "No, I prefer to go by foot."

And in the end, they said: "As you wish."

Or else they locked us forcibly into a car and took us back. On the path, the wheels of the cars crushed the grass, the flowers, the wild sweetbriar bushes, and the driver swore a lot, said that nobody thought of living in places like this. She said nothing and her eyes the color of tears looked into space.

The house looked very calm, very silent. We had on us something like the smell of gasoline. I went out a moment so the wind could carry it off, to listen again to the rustling of the willows in the wind, the water of the river, sometimes the foxes and birds hidden on the hill.

We ate a little and she cleaned the house, her feet, before going to bed. She fell asleep fast, very far away, and me, I couldn't sleep, I thought of what Antoine had proposed, of all those cars that came to crush the wild sweetbriar and nothing was the same anymore.

63

IT WAS nearly Christmas when Antoine came back. Enough time had passed that I almost never really thought anymore about all the terrible things that had happened in the spring and in the previous summer. It rained all the time. The earth and sky were full of water and mud. Day never broke. It was the time of year when she left in the night, in the first hours of the morning, the basket on her arm, the jute sack used as a hood on her head. She went to help kill the pig, or to force-feed the geese and ducks, or to kill and pluck the fatted geese and ducks and sell them the next day at the town market, and she stood waiting a long time in front of her poultry in the cold and damp among other women and merchants. At night she came home full of mud and wet with the greasy odor of pig or the sour smell of poultry and cows on her.

Some days, too, she went into the woods to make up bundles of kindling, and if it was a Thursday I followed her. At noon, she made a fire and heated our meal. If it was very cold, and it often was, the winter birds came to warm themselves by the fire while tranquilly chatting among themselves. I remember those gray days, the silence of the woods where the dead leaves crunched and the ax blows and cracking of branches echoed far in the distance, her and me in the woods cutting the branches, making the bundles, tying the kindling together, piling up the bundles. I remember her and me in the black dawns and dark twilights.

It was on one of those filthy Sunday nights that Antoine came back. Before seeing him, I heard muddy steps on the path. I ran to see because, ordinarily, nobody comes down these paths. As soon as I recognized Antoine in the light of the door, I said: "It's Antoine."

And my heart went crazy. I have a completely crazy heart sometimes.

She kept on with her work as if she hadn't heard and I wanted to say it again to warn her, but Antoine had already come in. He said: "Hello, Genie. Bring out the glasses, I have good wine."

And he pulled two dusty bottles out of his bag. We drank without saying anything and then he said: "That, now that is wine."

And he smacked his lips. He sat before the fire and talked about the rain that had turned the fields into swamps and that was becoming a problem for the cattle. He also talked about our house far from everything, at the end of a path that even animals wouldn't take, and the dampness of the house, you only had to look, the walls were crumbling with saltpeter, that's bad, and if a criminal came by, had she thought of that? No, you don't think about that, but if a criminal ever showed up, she could scream and scream, who would hear, nobody, and before anyone came to investigate, she would have had time to turn into white bones, exactly like that, and those crows, those foxes everywhere on the hill and sometimes they're rabid, and if they bite you, so long Charlie, it's over, and it's no life to go work for people who don't even say thank you and who pay you with three sausages or with a couple of apples, and even pigs don't begrudge apples, that's some life, and that, him, he wanted her to come live with him and keep his house and help a little in the barn and in the fields, it was an honest proposal and he wasn't forgetting that she came from the best family in the village, and him, if ever he could have a son he would be really happy because he was getting old, but she, she was young. That's the way he saw things, him, and those were honest things.

He stopped talking to give her time to reflect on his words and to respond. After a bit, as she said nothing, he said: "Listen, Genie. As for the little one, I've thought about it. If you really want, she'll go to school. But that will cost a lot."

She stayed for a moment in silence and then she said: "She will have scholarships."

And he said: "Yes. But the trips, morning and evening, that's extra, that and the cafeteria. Me, in my day I took my lunch to school. Now you've got to have the cafeteria."

She said: "She will be a boarder. She will come back on the holidays."

He said nothing more. Then, me, I talked about La Rochelle, that it was La Rochelle where I wanted to go, and I was thinking of the ocean, of the day when I would come back and get her to take her to see the ocean and maybe she would laugh.

She said: "La Rochelle, that's far away."

And me, I thought and I said: "But since I would only come back on the holidays."

Antoine had poured out more to drink, and the wine turned my head. He said, as he raised his glass: "To your health, Genie."

And he drank his glass in one go. He seemed very happy and she, her eyes were vague.

In the end, they decided that for the moment she would

go help him with the work and after the vacation, when I would be at La Rochelle, she would go live there.

And that's how things were.

When he had gone, I wanted to tell her that I was happy to study and to learn things about everything, that I wanted to go to La Rochelle to see the ocean because I had never seen the ocean, that one day, later, I would come back and get her and that I would take her to see the ocean and the lands where the vines climb to the sky, where the wild cyclamens grow in forests of acacias at the edge of the streams and you endlessly get lost while searching for their perfume.

I wanted to tell her all of that and that I loved her, that I loved her so much, and that me, I would prefer to stay forever in the old house, that me, I loved the willows crazy with the wind, the hill, the foxes that barked at night, that I wanted to stay there with her always. My heart was crazy as I thought of these things.

I went toward her. She washed the three glasses with her whole face far away. She said: "Go to sleep."

64

SHE DID what she'd said she'd do. If there was work at Antoine's, she went there and she also cooked for him. At night she ate with him and she brought food for me as in the days when she worked for the mayor. I waited for her very late, sitting near the door and I was afraid that she wouldn't come back, that she would decide to stay over there, in a real house, to leave me alone in the shack under the willows, and in my mind I begged her to come back and be with me a little.

If there was no work at Antoine's, she continued going to other people's places. At night they gave her more things. Sometimes she even brought back money and that's how she was able to buy proper clothes for me, for when I would be a boarder. She bought the things, she washed them, and she put them away in the trunk or the traveling bag she also had bought.

I watched her do it. I would have liked to say something to her because I understood that she was thinking of me, but she always wore her far-off expression and if I approached her to talk to her, she said: "Don't get in my hair."

Or: "Go to bed."

If it was nighttime.

Or: "Go do your homework."

This because we had decided that I would go to school in La Rochelle.

Sometimes, if it had been a long time since she'd gone to work for them, the people would come. They arrived with their cars in great splatters of mud mingled with curse words. They said: "It's been a long time since we've seen you, Crazy Genie."

She said nothing. They talked. They said this rain that wouldn't quit and how can you work when the fields are like lakes of mud, worse even. They talked about other people, about the baker who weighed the bread wrong, he puts the bread on the scale he adds a piece, small, and without giving you time to read the weight, he takes it all off and nobody dares say anything, ever, he steals, he steals nonstop. They talked about the butcher who sells cheap hams, country hams, and you know what country they come from, from Denmark, like I'm telling you, from Denmark, as if there weren't any here, country hams. They talked about other farms. They spoke at last about Antoine. He didn't look like much, to be sure, but with his sister, you know how he lived, with his sister, as if with a wife, exactly the same, and he even gave her a child and you know what they did with it, with the little one, they buried it in the dunghill, I'm telling you, and she died of this, you don't die for nothing. Other times they said that he had put it in an old cistern, other times in the ground underneath an apple tree. They always finished by saying: "He looks ordinary enough, to be sure, but you've got to be wary, defects run in a family."

She said nothing.

Sometimes, the people who came brought her things. Dried beans. Kidney beans and dried or frozen peas. Cabbages or celery. Wine. Sometimes even old unused furniture, nightstands, old, mismatched, worn-out chairs. She put them in piles behind the house and then, one night we burned them because there was nothing else to do.

She kept on going to work at Antoine's or at other people's places. Me, I went to school and, at night, waited for her to come back. I wondered what it was like, the ocean that meets the land, what the countries were like where the vines climb to the sky where the wild cyclamens call from deep forests of acacias.

65

THIS LAST summer in the old house might have been more beautiful than all the others. The sun and the rain were just as they should be and everyone was content, the people, the animals, and the plants.

She went out to work every day, at Antoine's or on other farms. She left early, in the first orange glimmers of the sun, she came back at night because she went every evening to make dinner for Antoine and to eat and she brought back food for me. Her face was always the same, pale and empty.

She didn't want me to go to the farms anymore. If I wanted to work with her, she said: "Study."

And I stuck around the house, studying in my schoolbooks for that year. One day, I picked up her book of flora, which was the book the grandfather had brought to her along with the bed when she was expecting me and had left the grandmother's house. In the book were the names of the plants at our place, even the ones, though they were so wild, on the foxes' hill. I was very happy because it was as if the people who had made the book had been thinking of the hill and the plants, and the plants became less neglected because people knew them and talked about them, by giving them a name.

Yes. That summer might have been more beautiful than the others.

One Sunday at the end of vacation, the grandfather came by. He brought out a bag of hazelnuts from his musette bag, gave it to me saying: "Eat, Marie."

She washed the clothes at the cistern. The grandfather went to her and said: "Eugénie, little one, they say you are going to go live at Antoine's."

She made no response and he said: "As for me, you do what you want. But there is your mother."

She stood up then, looked him full in the face, and said: "What mother."

And returned to her washing. The grandfather said again: "She's your mother, little one. She loved you in her way. Me I only came to warn you. She will come here because of Antoine."

He left and I looked at his stick, his musette bag, and his shoulder without an arm.

The grandmother arrived shortly after. She walked straight into the house. She was so big, tall, and full of authority that she filled the house. With her stick, she pointed at the old armoire, the bed, the table with legs eaten by damp and age and she said: "A Gypsy, that's what you've become. You have dishonored the finest family in the region. And now, not content with having produced a bastard, you are going to install yourself in the most sordid family in the village. But watch out. You know what everyone calls you, Crazy Genie. Crazy Genie, that's well chosen. I can have you shut up in the asylum. A madwoman at liberty, everyone looks at her. But a madwoman who's locked away, they forget her."

The grandmother left. My heart was full of terror.

66

ON THE eve of my departure for La Rochelle, she stayed with me at the house. My heart was crazy. She, she wore her habitual expression, her eyes far-off. She emptied the trunk and the bag, checked all the underwear, the clothes, everything, kept out a pleated skirt and a pullover that I would wear for the journey. Everything was new and pretty. I wanted to thank her, to tell her that me, I would prefer to stay there with her, always with her. But I said nothing, I knew it was no longer possible.

That night we stayed in front of the fire looking at nothing and I thought about things. Then I said: "I would like to know who my father is."

She said: "Shut up."

But I said: "I would like to know because I am going to leave and so are you."

For a moment she stayed with her eyes in the void, her aged hands hanging limply, remembering things of her own, perhaps. Then, she said: "It's Ernest, the mason."

Then I understood everything. Suddenly I felt all the old sadness of the earth upon me. I looked at her and began to cry hard, to cry and cry. She said: "You mustn't cry. It's not worth it."

And after a moment: "He wasn't bad. I didn't want to

marry him. So he lay in wait for me on the paths. He thought that would obligate me. That's all."

I went out to throw up in the grass. I stayed out in the night listening to the willows, the hill, and the blackness that fell from everywhere.

67

SHE HAD said: "You will come back at the holidays."

At Christmas, I couldn't go back. The high school closed and me, I couldn't leave. The headmistress said: "You have to leave. The high school must close at vacation."

And I: "It's not possible. I have no money."

With the money from the school's cooperative they bought me the train ticket, they gave me money for the bus. The train stopped for a long time in the countryside, and when it arrived at the station, late, all the buses had left. Then Pierre arrived and said: "I am Pierre."

And I: "I am Marie."

In the night, he told me about the islands perfumed with frangipani, of the blue shade of the sands, the caves of red birds, and the gardens of grapefruit where you fall asleep far away to the song of the wind in the casuarina trees on the hills, the jackals who cry at the moon on the edge of the desert.

Before leaving, he said: "I'll come get you at La Rochelle, and I will take you to the islands where I was born."

68

NOBODY was waiting for me anywhere. I went to Antoine's to see if she was there. She was there and my heart, seeing her, began to go crazy I was so happy. She looked at me and said: "It's you, Marie."

Antoine said nothing. I explained very quickly why I'd had to come back, that it wasn't my fault, that they wanted at all costs to close the school at Christmas, and that they didn't know what to do with me, that it wasn't my fault really. And then, I was so cold all over, I started to cry. She said: "You mustn't cry."

And then: "It's good that you came."

I saw that her eyes were not so far away.

I said that I didn't know where to go because during all those months I thought that maybe the grandmother had had her locked up, that these were unbearable things, and, in my mind, I remembered all those dreams that I had almost every night, they came to get her, they put her in the jute bag and carried her off like that, and she screamed, me, I ran, I ran behind her as fast as my little legs would carry me, because in my dream I was always very little, I called her, I called her and the doors closed I didn't see her anymore and I stayed all alone in unknown streets and she, behind the doors, she screamed, because of things they were doing to her.

Then Antoine said that I might well never have seen her

again, but that he had been smarter than all the others. Because everyone had agreed to say she was crazy and to have her locked up, all the people, and this because they didn't want her to go live with him, Antoine, and they had reason, a worker like that, one that you don't pay, that you don't even thank, you don't find that growing on trees, and you know what they found, to prove she was crazy, it was that she didn't demand a real salary. And the doctor, he too agreed, he never had forgiven her for the insult she gave him when she didn't want to go work for him. They all were in agreement, to say she was crazy, now, all of a sudden. But he, Antoine, he had got the better of all of them. Yes. Because when he had found out she was going to have a baby, he had decided to marry her and now, it was he who was master, and he would have a son, and nobody could do anything about it.

He was very happy. She, her eyes were less vague and I understood why.

69

SHE DIDN'T work on the farms anymore. At Antoine's, she worked little. He didn't want her to do heavy work, or to milk the cows, for fear that a cow might kick her in the belly.

"It doesn't take much," Antoine said.

You just pull too hard on one teat and the cow gives you a nasty kick. He wanted a handsome, healthy son. He had decided he would give him his father's name, Louis.

I didn't go work at people's houses either.

Antoine said, "They wanted to lock her up so she wouldn't come here."

She said, "Study."

And I studied. I also helped her in the house. I stayed near her, loving her in silence. She no longer said anything to make me move away. She never spoke of the child who was going to be born, however, I knew well that it was for him that she had those bright eyes. One day, she said, "When you were born, I was still very little."

And I remembered that she was seventeen years old when I was born. I remembered the mason lying in wait between the hedges, and also how I ran behind her as fast as my little legs would carry me because I was afraid she might lose me, that she might abandon me or simply that she would forget me there.

She stayed in Antoine's house, and the house was clean and orderly, and Antoine spoke incessantly of his son, he would take him on the tractor, he would install a little seat just for him, they would go to the fair together, they would sit in a café like the rich and they would drink a glass together, they would go hunting for mushrooms, he would study and become an agronomist, just like that.

Sometimes she said: "He will be tiny."

And he: "They grow fast."

And me, my heart was full of tears.

I went once more to the old house under the willows. I tried for a while to pull out the nettles that had sprung from the ground at the foot of the walls, and then I gave up because my hands began to burn and because I thought no doubt she would never go back there, and it wasn't worth it. Then I amused myself by following the paths of the foxes in the grass. They all led to the hill of white sand or to the river. The hill was bare, with its bare trees. I wondered if the foxes still came barking outside the house at night. In the house, everything was there, the old bed, the table limping with age, the big armoire, and the fireplace with very old ashes. I thought of the times when she would say: "And me, I've had nothing."

I listened for a moment to the naked voice of the willows in the wind.

When I came back, she said: "You mustn't go back there."

And then: "You are still little."

Then I put my face in her neck, as in the past, when she would finally take me into her arms and talk to me.

70

AT LA ROCHELLE, the courtyard of the school was planted with chestnut trees. Often, I climbed up onto the portico of the courtyard. I would look at the ocean. There were the chestnut trees and, beyond that, the ocean. If I lay back on the portico, I could see the tops of the chestnut trees in the sky and above them, the black waters of the ocean.

In the blue hours of dawn, the pigeons perched on the edges of the windows and cooed.

Later, in springtime, the chestnut trees flourished their gentle clusters in the sky. I thought of the paulownia at the grandmother's house that I would never see again. Leaning against a white chestnut tree, a red chestnut tree slowly flourished its clusters. In the daytime, in the night, the white chestnut tree rocked the red chestnut tree in its branches. I looked and I thought of Pierre who had said: "I will come get you at La Rochelle."

I dreamed that he would gather me in his branches like a tree. Much later, Pierre wrote: "You are my gentle country beside the wandering ocean." And he was my ocean.

He wrote: "You are my sunlit land."

And he was my tree.

71

IN THE month of July, when I came back, little Louis had been born two months before. I thought I wouldn't like him, but I was mistaken. I loved him at once like I loved her. I took him everywhere with me, in my arms, and he, he slept, quietly, indoors as well as outdoors. Antoine was disappointed to see that a baby was so small, but consoled himself by saying: "He grows quickly, like a true son of Antoine."

And soon, he would take him onto the tractor where he had installed the little seat. She didn't say anything. But as soon as the baby cried, she gave him the breast, and the entire time he nursed, she looked at him, and me, I understood in those moments that no matter what I did, she and little Louis, that was a world I had never known. I was not sad, because little Louis was so small and so beautiful that you couldn't help loving him and rejoicing to see him loved and loving.

The school terms followed one another, intercut with vacations at Antoine's, close to her.

At the high school, I still climbed onto the portico to see, beyond the chestnut trees, the green waters of the ocean. In springtime, I lay beneath the chestnut trees like in the past under the grandmother's big paulownia, I watched the white chestnut tree rock the red chestnut tree in its branches. I thought of Pierre who was supposed to come and get me and who had not yet come.

Little Louis grew and in summer he walked. I loved him and he loved me. I remember that, in the nights, in front of the setting sun, toward which he stretched out his hands, I would make up a story for him. I told him: "I will bring you a big white kangaroo and we will leap over the mountains riding on the big kangaroo, far away to lands where the vines climb into the sky and the suns devour people's faces."

Little Louis didn't understand but he looked at me, his big eyes open wide, and then he laughed because we were playing at galloping like a big kangaroo.

I remember those happy evenings and little Louis.

Then there was that Christmas.

I came back and little Louis was already a year and a half. When I arrived, she said: "The grandfather is going to die."

And at once I said: "I'm going to go see him."

I brought out the bicycle that had a little seat behind on the luggage rack. Antoine said: "Take the little one. Show them how handsome he is."

And it was true that he was handsome, my little brother.

He had black hair full of curls and big green eyes that looked straight at you, and above all, he was always laughing. He wasn't afraid to go to her, to throw himself into her arms and love her. All the joy he had in living gave him a happy face and happy eyes beholding the world. Me, I loved him.

72

HARDLY having arrived at the grandmother's house, I saw, because of the cars, that the uncles, the aunts, the boy cousins, and the girl cousins were there. I thought that was normal because the grandfather was sick. I also thought of the grandmother who would say as soon as I walked in: "She is coming to spy."

But I went in anyway. I wanted to see my grandfather, who was going to die, my grandfather, who sometimes lifted his eyes from his books full of old kings who had been dead forever or had gone crazy, nobody knew why, and who gave me walnuts, hazelnuts, or an apple saying: "Eat, little one."

And afterward I could throw the apple core or the shells into the grandmother's well and that was pointless because the well hadn't been in use for ages, but I did it all the same.

But I should have fled instead of going in. Truly, with all my strength, I should have fled.

I came in with little Louis and I said at once, so everyone would understand: "I've come to see the grandfather."

The grandmother led me to the bedroom. The grandfather was in his bed. He said: "It's you, little one. I was expecting you."

And I felt full of happiness.

I said to him: "I brought little Louis. He looks like you."

And it was true. He looked at him and said: "He's a handsome little child. Truly a handsome little child. You will tell her so."

And then he said: "Leave him with the cousins. This isn't a sight for him, here."

I led little Louis to the cousins, in the grandmother's big kitchen.

From the bedroom, the grandfather talked about her. She had been a good and beautiful little girl who always sang and laughed. She had been sweet and happy, and everyone had loved her except her mother, who only loved her sons. And then that misfortune had come. But he was happy that Antoine had taken her into his home and now she had a beautiful child. Me, I said that the little one looked like him and that she, she was happy, that her eyes were no longer far away like before when the two of us were in the old house, and my heart was crazy at the memory of all that. The grandfather said: "Don't be sad, Marie. Now there's the little one."

Then I thought of Louis whom I had left with the cousins. I left the bedroom very quickly to go find him. He wasn't in the kitchen anymore, and neither were the cousins. I heard the laughter from the cellar. I ran. They were holding little Louis under a barrel and making him drink wine from the open tap. As soon as they saw me, they let go of little Louis and ran away, leaving the tap open. I took my little brother, I tapped him on the back so he could get his breath back. He was drenched in wine, and very pale. He whimpered softly.

On the road, I pedaled and pedaled and pedaled. I was afraid because of the wine he had drunk and because he was all wet in the chill of Christmastime. Arriving at Antoine's

I told him everything. She had changed him, warmed him, tried to make him throw up, but he hadn't vomited. He whimpered. He was so pale that he looked green.

I said: "We must call the doctor."

She said: "He won't come."

And I remembered that she hadn't wanted to go work for him and that he had tried to have her committed. She held little Louis against her and sang a sad song so he could calm down and go to sleep.

I got back on my bicycle and I went to the village to tell the doctor. I explained to him that little Louis was very sick, that he had to come quickly.

He said: "Oh yes. It's the son of Crazy Genie. I heard about that."

I said: "It's little Louis."

And again I said that he was very sick, that he had to come quickly to see him. He explained that he wasn't too sure when he would come by, he had urgent calls far off in the countryside. But he would come, it was certain.

I left, my heart full of hatred. When he arrived the next day, little Louis was dead. His little face was the color of ivory and his black hair full of curls like a halo. She kept rocking him in her arms while singing that song from olden days that tells of clocks that weep the tears of a child.

When night came, Antoine took his cans of gasoline and went to burn down the grandmother's house and barn. Only the barn burned. The cows mooed far off in the countryside.

When they took little Louis from her arms to put him in the coffin, she went to get his Sunday shoes. She polished them, made them shine with the woolen cloth, polished them again and made them gleam. She also ironed his best dress. Then she washed, combed her hair, put on a dress and shoes. She sat next to little Louis, hands clasped, and waited. If Antoine came into the bedroom and told her to rest a bit, she went out, sat on the bench in front of the door in her well-ironed dress and polished shoes, and she waited.

73

THEY BURIED little Louis the same day as the grandfather. Around little dead Louis there were: Antoine, her, and me. At the exit of the cemetery, the police were waiting for Antoine. We went back to the house. She changed her clothes, cleaned the dirty and disorderly house, tended the fowls and the cows, as usual, exactly as usual.

When she had finished all those chores, she wandered for a while in the farmyard and in the house. She settled herself in front of the fire, emptied the damp straw from her rubber clogs. Next, she soaked her feet in a basin of warm water before cleaning the cracks in her heels with a matchstick. I watched her and waited, sitting by the fireplace. I would have liked to go up to her, to tell her how much I still loved her, how much I loved her. But her face was pallid, so far away from everything. She made herself a little presentable, put her dress from the morning back on, her polished shoes, and headed off toward the old house under the willows.

They pulled her out of the cistern with a hoist.

The grandmother said, when I told her: "I was quite right to want them to lock her up."

They buried her by little Louis. That day I was all alone with her.

For some time, the people of the village talked about her

a bit. They would tell their stories and always end by saying: "It wasn't for nothing that we called her Crazy Genie."

Let her sleep I tell you let her sleep
    or I vow that the earth will crack open,
That everything henceforth
Will be finished between the moss
    and the coffin . . .

Let let her sleep
Leave the great oaks around her bed
Don't chase from her room this humble
Half-erased daisy
Let let her sleep.

—Robert Desnos,
from "Passé le pont" in
Les Ténèbres

OTHER NEW YORK REVIEW CLASSICS

For a complete list of titles, visit www.nyrb.com.

CLAUDE ANET Ariane, A Russian Girl
SORAYA ANTONIUS The Lord
HANNAH ARENDT Rahel Varnhagen: The Life of a Jewish Woman
HONORÉ DE BALZAC The Lily in the Valley
POLINA BARSKOVA Living Pictures
ROSALIND BELBEN The Limit
ANDRÉ BRETON Nadja
DINO BUZZATI The Betwitched Bourgeois: Fifty Stories
CRISTINA CAMPO The Unforgivable and Other Writings
CAMILO JOSÉ CELA The Hive
EILEEN CHANG Time Tunnel: Stories and Essays
FRANÇOIS-RENÉ DE CHATEAUBRIAND Memoirs from Beyond the Grave, 1815–1830
AMIT CHAUDHURI A New World
LUCILLE CLIFTON Generations: A Memoir
RACHEL COHEN A Chance Meeting: American Encounters
COLETTE Chéri *and* The End of Chéri
JEAN ECHENOZ Command Performance
FERIT EDGÜ The Wounded Age *and* Eastern Tales
BENITO PÉREZ GÁLDOS Miaow
MAVIS GALLANT The Uncollected Stories of Mavis Gallant
ROBERT GLÜCK Jack the Modernist
PIERRE GUYOTAT Idiocy
RICHARD HELL Godlike
HENRY JAMES On Writers and Writing
SIEGFRIED KRACAUER Ginster
LUIS MARTÍN-SANTOS Time of Silence
JOHN McGAHERN The Pornographer
AUGUSTO MONTERROSO The Rest is Silence
ELSA MORANTE Lies and Sorcery
MANUEL MUJICA LÁINEZ Bomarzo
PIER PAOLO PASOLINI Boys Alive
KONSTANTIN PAUSTOVSKY The Story of a Life
HENRIK PONTOPPIDAN A Fortunate Man
MARCEL PROUST Swann's Way
BARBARA PYM The Sweet Dove Died
JONATHAN SCHELL The Village of Ben Suc
ANNA SEGHERS The Dead Girls' Class Trip
ELIZABETH SEWELL The Orphic Voice
ROGER SHATTUCK The Forbidden Experiment: The Story of the Wild Boy of Aveyron
JEAN STAFFORD Boston Adventure
ITALO SVEVO A Very Old Man
MAGDA SZABÓ The Fawn
ELIZABETH TAYLOR Mrs Palfrey at the Claremont
SUSAN TAUBES Lament for Julia
GABRIELE TERGIT Effingers
MICHEL TOURNIER Friday
YŪKO TSUSHIMA Woman Running in the Mountains
KONSTANTIN VAGINOV Goat Song
PAUL VALÉRY Monsieur Teste
MARKUS WERNER The Frog in the Throat
VIRGINIA WOOLF Mrs. Dalloway: The First-Edition Text with the Author's Revisions